Sha

A Blue Duck Social Club Novel

by K. R. Morden

Copyright © 2025

Kenneth R. Morden

All rights reserved

The characters and events portrayed in this book are fictitious. Any similarity to real persons, living or dead, is coincidental and not intended by the author.

No part of this book may be reproduced, or stored in a retrieval system, or transmitted in any form or by any means, electronic, mechanical, photocopying, recording, or otherwise, without express written permission of the publisher.

ISBN: 9798282919042

Printed in Canada

Chapter 1

Marg O'Toole paused briefly in the vestibule of the Blue Duck Tavern and grabbed the last copy of the free Port Detour Times from the rack. The large wooden front door closed behind her, plunging the bar room into near darkness, except for the lights over the bar in the centre. As if in a stage spotlight, Kendrick Overland's body appeared from below the counter where he had been arranging the wine bottles. Her body tensed as it always did when seeing Kendrick. The horrible incident of forty years ago re-surfaced in her mind's eye. She forced her feet to move forward.

"Yo Marg," he called out, waving in her general direction. "I didn't know anyone was here. I'll turn on the lights. What'll you have, Marg? Champagne or the '84 Chablis?" He laughed uproariously at his own remark.

"White wine. I'll sit over there," she said, pointing and moving to a large round corner table. She sat down and spread the Times in front of her.

There were four break and enters, (a crime wave, said the writer) and the Port Detour Wildcats won their fifth baseball game in a row. But it was the top headline that commanded attention. It read, 'Local election campaigning in full swing' and featured pictures of every candidate from mayor down to school trustee. Solid looking citizens, every one of them. Election day was four weeks away.

A glass of white wine suddenly appeared on the table. "Sorry, the champagne machine broke just as I was going to pour your drink, Marg. I'll give you a rain cheque for next time." Again, the uproarious laugh from Kendrick.

Marg glanced at the sixty-ish man and mentally recoiled at what she saw. But it wasn't his clothes that caused the reaction. She saw a teenage high school classmate who either couldn't recall, or chose not to recall, what he had done to her at their graduation party. The situation today was far removed from that time, forty years ago, and it had nothing to do with the way they dressed.

Marg's dress style was exactly like the relaxed lifestyle of the Blue Duck Club members. She wore white runners, jeans and a loose-fitting light red sweater. Unlike the other members, every piece sported a designer label.

In Kendrick's case, he no doubt believed he was the picture of fashion, thought Marg. How else to explain the lack of embarrassment with the clash of colours and the tight-fitting pants? Give him credit, though. He appeared trim and fit, and his greyish brown hair was still full and wavy. But after two years of listening to his verbal pomposity, her brain reacted to it like fingernails on a chalkboard.

After her brief perusal, she turned back to her reading, not acknowledging Kendrick or the glass of wine. Absorbing the words was now impossible. Her face was blank, her eyes unfocussed, her mind reviewing the details from forty years ago. They were as clear today as then. Kendrick had been the sicko, ably abetted by his brother, Everet.

In her role as a criminal defence lawyer, she was asked with regularity if she knew which clients were guilty. "None. They're all innocent."

This was different. There certainly wasn't any question in her mind whether Kendrick and his brother were guilty. Forty years ago, she was the one who had been victimized. Not that Kendrick seemed to remember.

The bang of the front door interrupted her thoughts. Bright sunlight flooded in, silhouetting the person coming through. He paused for an instant as his eyes adjusted to the darker interior, then made a beeline for Marg's table and pulled out a chair. There was no response from Marg.

"Hi Marg, you look like you're someplace else," said Rey Rey, as he sat down beside Marg. He said it with a straight face, no emotion showing, acquired from a lifetime of commiserating with his clients. Rey Rey, the retired undertaker, was as straight as Marg. Life was serious business. Marg's dress mode provided confirmation, not so much the slight man now seated opposite her.

"Hi Rey Rey," said Marg, finally looking up at the man in the tropical shirt and cargo shorts. A small smile appeared on her face. A year ago, Rey Rey wouldn't be caught dead in his current attire.

"You're looking good. You're also early. What's new?"

"Well, I hear my old business is dead, or at least I think it is. Do you know I've been retired for exactly one year today, so I don't hear a lot about it? But I know people keep dying whether or not I'm there."

He laughed at his idea of a humorous comment. Marg didn't and moved her chair over to make room for two more patrons. Everyone at the table was early for the weekly meeting of the Blue Duck Social Club. As they sat down, Marg held up the Port Detour Times and said, "Does anyone know who's running in this election?" There were blank stares from everyone.

Gail and Forest ignored the question, and both waved towards the bar. Kendrick acknowledged the wave with a thumbs up. He obviously knew what the regulars wanted. He placed the drinks on a serving tray and moved to the table from the bar area. His movement was more swagger than walking. The logo splattered across his black T-shirt in bright yellow read 'Detour Beer, Worth The Trip', further highlighting his light green silk jacket and white slacks. He held a bowl of chips in his right hand, drinks for Forest and Gail in his left. He placed the drinks in front of the two patrons and turned his head to Rey Rey, anticipating a drink order.

Instead, Gail spoke up. "Hey Kendrick, could you pick up that napkin on the floor? I want to see those pants split."

A broad smile appeared on his face.

Rey Rey added, "Club soda, please."

Kendrick was back within a few minutes. "Here's the consolation prize." He set down a bowl of pretzels.

Speaking to no one in particular, he added, "Anybody lose money yesterday?" No one said anything. He continued, "I did. Big time. The market was down one hundred points." He shrugged. "Oh well, easy come, easy go."

There was no response from the four people at the table, only stares. Kendrick gave up and moved towards the bar. "If you need anything, just raise your hand," he called out as he left. "Other than the washrooms," he laughed, "You don't need my permission."

Gail waved her glass at the others and with a light smile, asked, "Does anybody wonder what he did for the past forty years? Do we know any more about him than we did two years ago?" She took a sip of her chardonnay and asked, "Where did he get his money from? All he's got is chutzpa, and that doesn't pay well."

"I think he got paid off by his last wife. She had a lot of money, or at least she did until she married Kendrick," volunteered Rey Rey.

Everyone laughed and nodded in agreement, remembering a previous discussion when they had concluded Kendrick's career was likely more a hustler or con man than a clothing salesman. Marg silently agreed. It was so easy seeing him in that role based on her knowledge of his morals and sense of entitlement.

Gail spoke up. Her appearance screamed academia, English style. Her post grad education in England also included the acquisition of a faux English accent and some English slang words. She was a slight woman and her hair stuck out in places where it had escaped from the series of hair clips marching to the back of her head. Unlike the unruly hair, her pant suit was severe, brown, pin-striped, and a perfect fit.

"What a hoot. Imagine the bloke selling bathing suits from his truck, travelling around Northern Ontario for forty years? Forest, you said he had a successful business. My ass. He must have been involved in something illegal. Drugs maybe?"

She continued to make eye contact with the other people seated at the large round table, pausing for a moment on the face of her live-in partner, Forest Green, and broke into a smile. She loved this setting, so unlike the academic world she had retired from. The bar, the table, the oak-panelled walls shared the same thing–all were old and well-preserved. Just like the people. The table sat in a corner of the large barroom, out of earshot of the few other patrons. Gail raised and waved her glass as if to punctuate the point.

Forest, sitting to Gail's left, took a sip of his beer and frowned at her statement. "You don't know anything about him, Gail. Where are you getting this from?

The group around the table knew Gail, the professor, didn't take to being challenged, and all conversation stopped to better hear what Forest might say.

"He kept in touch with me regularly over the last forty years. We're good friends. I know him better than anyone around this table. The only thing he worked at was his mobile bathing suit business. You saw his van, the one with the movie star in a bikini painted on the side. That was his advertisement, showroom, office and his living space when he was on the road."

Like Gail, he made his appeal for agreement with a wave of his glass. "The business was a roaring success."

Gail wasn't finished. "Forest, you're so naïve. How do you know this? Is that what he told you? Why should you believe anything he says? Just look at the stories he's told us over the past two years. You know, Forest, as a professor, I had to verify everything I was told. Kendrick's stories are fantasy. I find most of them hard to believe."

"On the contrary, my dear," Forest said, uncharacteristically trying to lighten the moment. He pushed back the few strands of hair crossing his shiny scalp. "I may be naïve compared to everyone else around this table, but forty years at Smith & Sons exposed me to many types of people, and Kendrick is a good guy. I believe him when he says he's wealthy."

Gail frowned, gave Forest a squinted look, leaned forward to pick up her wineglass, and immediately put it down. It was empty. She raised her arm and waved at the bar, hoping to catch Kendrick's eye.

Unlike most taverns, the bar was positioned in the middle of the large room and was configured in an oval shape, like a racetrack. Suspended from the ceiling area over the oval bar were racks and racks of glasses of all shapes and sizes, brightly lit from the lights in the ceiling, illuminating the entire bar area.

Kendrick Overland looked up from wiping the dark wooden bar surface, showed a big grin and waved back, completely unaware they were talking about him. He motioned upward with his thumb. Gail nodded. She then directed her gaze to another tablemate.

"Rey Rey, what do you think? Is Kendrick on the up and up? We haven't seen him for forty years and then he shows up without explanation. Don't you think that's suspicious?"

Rey Rey Gonsalves' forever sympathetic face appeared frozen. He also wasn't used to being asked his opinion. Dead people don't converse that much.

He put his glass of beer down, looked around the table and in a flat voice said, "I think you're right, Gail. He didn't gain all his wealth from his business. How many women in Northern Ontario need a bathing suit? Maybe he was a drug dealer? He had a perfect cover. Nobody could question his moving around every city and town in the north." In his slow, ponderous way of speaking, he added, "Do you know something else?"

Marg was noticeably quiet during the verbal exchange. She stopped looking at Kendrick behind the bar and her face brightened as she mentally rejoined the group, asking, "No Rey Rey, we know nothing else, but I'm sure you're going to tell us. Is this gossip from your funeral buddies in the north? Do you guys have an underground newsletter or something?"

"No Marg, it's just a thought I had. Why did Kendrick come back to Port Detour after so many years away? Also, why did he leave?"

"He said it was time to retire," said Forest. "But I really don't know why he left, unless it was to find a better job." All conversation stopped as Kendrick approached the table and, with a flourish, set a glass of white wine down in front of Gail. "Here, lovely lady, this is for you. Is there anything else your obedient servant Kendrick can bring you?" The words sounded phony, but Kendrick pulled it off with a broad smile and a friendly sounding voice.

Marg spoke up. "Here's the man himself, people. Let's ask him. Kendrick, why did you come back to Port Detour? Even better, why did you leave? Life in the north can't be attractive for a guy like you. In high school, I remember you as a party animal. I imagine you still like the brights lights, the fast women and the nightlife."

He squinted his eyes as he replied, looking directly at Marg. "Ooh, here's the third degree from the famous criminal lawyer. Marg, aren't you retired? But you're partially right." Then his smile returned, and he said in a loud voice, staring firmly at Marg for a few seconds. "And I still like fast women."

Marg rose from her seat, her head almost at Kendrick's level. She stared at him and her hand moved ever so slightly, as if her next move was to grab him where he was most vulnerable.

"Take it back, Kendrick."

He made no move nor said anything for a moment, then he must have suddenly remembered Marg's career and the sleazy characters she represented. Characters who would have taught her a few self defence moves. "Sorry, Marg. I didn't intend it the way it came out."

Marg sat down; eyes still locked on Kendrick's. All the other people at the table were staring at Marg. She slowly moved her head, looked around, and smiled.

Kendrick feigned unconcern, smiling, "Tell me, what's your reason for asking about me?"

Nobody spoke, so Marg continued. "Well, Kendrick, all of us know what each of us did after we graduated from Port Detour High. As for you, you're a mystery man. Forty years in Northern Ontario?"

Kendrick smoothed his hair, stood more upright, flashed his eyes around the table, and his smile became broader.

"All of you know the story. I got sent to jail before I graduated from high school. That's why I wasn't in your graduating class. Do you want to know why?"

Everybody looked a little embarrassed, held their eyes down and closely studied their drinks. Nobody wanted to be seen prying into someone's private life. In their own minds, they could hardly wait.

"Sure you do. I'll be back. I gotta serve some drinks. Give me five." He turned and walked back to the bar, leaving the group looking at each other silently. Marg spoke to no one in particular. "What's he hiding? We asked about the forty years, not what happened before."

Chapter 2

In the middle of Marg's question, a tall dark man wearing a brightly coloured dashiki and Kufi hat and sporting frizzy pure white hair, walked up to the table with a fresh beer in his hand. In any other setting, he would have attracted attention immediately as he entered the room. This group never noticed him coming in, except Marg, who was always fascinated with Dakari's dress. He claimed it was his homage to life as an artist.

"I'm here. Am I holding up the shareholders' meeting or the election gossip? What's the serious discussion, guys?" he said to his high school classmates.

"Hi Dakari," said Marg. "We've been talking about what Kendrick did since he left Port Detour forty years ago. Forest says he ran his own business selling women's' bathing suits. His van was also his showroom, and he travelled all over Northern Ontario. Some of us think it's a crock of shit. Grab a chair and sit down. "

"Well, well. Doesn't that raise a lot of questions? I can't imagine the market in Northern Ontario is very large for women's bathing suits, unless it's to wear in a sauna in the winter." He paused and frowned. "No, that can't be right. This isn't Nigeria. You wear nothing in a sauna, do you? Maybe he sold to cross dressers." He roared with laughter at the thought. "It would be like a sheep in wolf's clothing, or something like that. "

As if on cue, Kendrick appeared and stood in front of the five people. Previously distracted by his clothing choices, Marg now noticed his accessories. Compared to other men she knew, Kendrick was an anti-fashion statement. He was a barnyard rooster amongst the peacocks. Port Detour must have the sleaziest dressed bartender in the country, thought Marg.

The accessories were brilliant but too bright to be real, including a gold watch with the name Rolex prominently displayed on its face. Three gold-coloured chains hung from his neck over his black beer slogan T-shirt. He leaned over and placed his hands on the table between Marg and Gail.

"OK, here's the why. It all started with my older brother, Everet. I don't think anyone here knew him. He was three years ahead of us at PDH."

Everyone nodded in agreement, except Marg. Suddenly, she jumped in.

"Kendrick, we all knew that you were sent away to a reform school. We didn't know any details other than you stole something. You're saying Everet set you up?"

"Damn right he did. The year I was sixteen, I went away to summer camp for two weeks. Dad asked Everet to deliver my papers while I was away. About a week after I returned, the cops showed up at our door. They had received several complaints that people on my route had their houses broken into and things were missing. It didn't take them long to figure out that all the houses were on my paper route. Mom and Dad met them at the front door, and the cops explained the situation. The cops knew Dad. You know how it is in Port Detour. Everyone knows everyone else. He called Everet and me to the living room and asked one cop to repeat the information they had. I remember distinctly what happened next."

Everyone was leaning forward now.

"One cop asked. 'Walt, do you think we can take a look at the boys' bedrooms?' Dad said, 'Sure.'"

"Everet and I followed them into his bedroom, and then mine. It didn't take long. They found nothing in his room. My room was a different story. They found stolen goods, credit cards and cash. Everet was quick with an explanation. He swore to the cops he'd seen me bring all the loot back to our house. The cops believed him. Mom believed her favourite son. I was sent away for two years to a juvenile detention facility. Everet got off scot free and when I was released, he was long gone, off on another scam I suppose."

Forest asked, "But what has that to do with your forty years up north?"

"No one wanted anything to do with me and no one wanted to give an ex-con a job. I was ostracized. There was nothing for me in Port Detour, so I left. It's as simple as that, no great mystery. I was still a kid and the thought of going further away than two hundred kilometres was scary. I picked Sudbury in Northern Ontario, where nobody knew me, and I didn't have a reputation. "

Marg had edged closer and by the time Kendrick finished, her elbows were on the table and she was gazing intently at him. She opened up her hand and pointed at him. "But Kendrick, what about the forty years?"

Kendrick suddenly looked over at the bar and stood up. "Gotta go. I've got another thirsty customer over there. I'll be back." He raised his arm and yelled out, "I'm coming!"

As he fled, Marg yelled after him in a loud voice, "We still haven't heard about the forty years, Kendrick." His arm raised in acknowledgment, but the flight to the bar continued.

As soon as Kendrick was out of earshot, Forest put up his hand as if he were in a classroom.

"I'm bothered by your question, Marg. What Kendrick did during the last forty years is his business. Let's leave him alone. Why do you want to know, anyway?"

Marg gave Forest a withering stare. "Are you kidding, Forest? The guy is running the Blue Duck Tavern. He's in charge of everything– the money, the treatment of customers, safety, security and more. And who owns the Blue Duck Tavern, Forest?"

"We do, Marg. We're all shareholders in the tavern. So what? So is Kendrick. He's not going to do anything to affect his investment, is he?"

"People who are broke do strange things, Forest. What if he's desperate? He's now got the perfect opportunity. And I know he's slippery." She let that sink in, glancing at everyone around the table. Her voice firmed up, as though Kendrick was now a felon she was defending. She wasn't finished.

"How much money do you have, Forest? One million, three million, more? If a patron slips because Kendrick didn't clean the floor and is injured, who pays when he sues? The insurance company will go after us, the shareholders. We'll be the ones who eventually pay. And that includes you, and you and you," she said, turning to face each person at the table.

"How would you like to be broke at our age? Being a greeter at Walmart doesn't pay much."

There was complete silence around the table.

"Anyway, when you hire an employee, you always know, or should know, what his history was. In this case, is he even qualified for the job or is his experience solely on the drinking side? He says he ran his own business. We don't know that other than his verbal statement. Other than his brother's accusation, was he ever in trouble with the law?"

She continued. "Two years ago, nobody checked with me. I heard later we needed a manager quickly, so we didn't even check his references. The insurance company would have a ball with that one."

Dakari Smith, who had been following the conversation without interjecting, studied Marg intently.

"Marg, I detect something here. Do you know something about Kendrick the rest of us don't? Also, why have you waited two years to bring this up?"

Marg didn't miss a beat. She instantly answered, "What I know is we have a convicted felon in charge of our tavern. I don't like it and I want something done about it. Forest, you're the President. Fix this."

"I don't know what I can do, Marg. He's an employee and has done nothing wrong. It would be wrongful dismissal and it would cost us a fortune."

Dakari frowned and looked directly at Marg. "Marg, what do you know about Kendrick the rest of us don't? What's the bee in your bonnet? Why are you so adamant he's got to go?"

Marg's eyes narrowed, and her face hardened. "Something happened to me in high school, which I'll never forget. It involved Kendrick. It still bothers me and it's made an enormous difference in my life. I don't want to talk about it. It's best left for another time."

Gail spoke up. "Hey Marg, you're almost like Kendrick. Why the secrecy? Why haven't you told anybody, especially when Kendrick showed up two years ago?"

"There was no need to tell, Gail. I'd already kept quiet for forty years. But something happened yesterday." Her hand tightened around her wineglass and her voice volume decreased noticeably.

"His brother is back," she whispered. "I saw Everet downtown yesterday. He's as much of a sleazeball as Kendrick, don't you know?" Her composure disappeared for an instant, her words trying to get out.

"Those brothers have to be plotting something. God knows what it is. Right now, my problem from forty years ago hasn't gone away. It's back."

The rest of the group drew their chairs closer to the table. Marg looked at them, wishing the juries and judges evaluating her cases showed the same interest when she was defending an accused. Personal and private problems trumped everything in most people's minds.

She continued. "Seeing those two again is frightening. Don't worry, I'll get over it, but it has brought back memories of what happened. I'll explain later once I find out what those two are up to."

The others looked at each other in disappointment, but the promise of a revelation in the future was some solace. Marg had one last closing remark.

"They're trouble, everyone, big trouble. Take it from me, I know. End of discussion." She downed her wine, got up, and walked rapidly to the exit, leaving her perfume scent as the only evidence of her time at the table.

"Just when we were getting to the good part," said Dakari, expressing everyone's disappointment. "Trouble," she had said, "big trouble."

The group realized there couldn't be any further revelations, but everyone understood Marg's forecast of the future.

Their drinks unfinished, they were reluctant to say their social time had come to the end. Gail looked around the table. "So, what else should we worry about?"

"There's not much happening in this town, Gail. The only thing I'm worried about is the price of eggs. They aren't cheap anymore. "

"I know," said Rey Rey, "we have a municipal election coming up. I've always heard that the current councillors are on the take. Do you think it's true?"

Dakari leaned forward on the table. "If they are," he said, a malevolent grin on this face, "we should nominate our retired police chief for mayor. Emile would have a ball, he'd be the fox guarding the henhouse."

Gail laughed, "I think you have your metaphors mixed up, Dakari."

Dakari frowned. "What's wrong? Everyone knows that saying. What I really mean is, we should elect people with integrity."

"That's very difficult to find," said Gail. "We need somebody who hasn't lived here for long. Somebody who isn't one of the 'old boys.'

Chapter 3

They sat there trying to absorb what Marg had said about the two people.

Dakari spoke up. "Marg doesn't speculate. She knows. I believe her when she says Everet's return is even more troublesome than her terrible experience involving him, whatever it is. And he's been away for forty years. He's just like a newcomer, except he's one of us."

"He's not one of us, Dakari. God knows what he's been up to. We haven't seen or heard from him for decades," said Forest. "We don't know a damn thing about him."

Rey Rey asked, "Other than Marg, does anyone remember Everet? I certainly don't. Marg doesn't seem to have a very high opinion of him, does she?"

Gail's faux English side came out. "Blimey, just who is this guy? Should we be locking our doors at night?" She said it in jest, but with an element of fear evident. "And what about Kendrick? All we know is what he's done for the past two years. We're missing eighteen years. At least he has killed none of us." Everyone was silent as she continued. "I could be wrong. Let's have a head count."

Her attempt at humour fell flat. Nobody laughed. The thought occurred to her she may have stayed too long at the university. "Marg says the two of them are trouble. Where does that leave us?"

Rey Rey volunteered a thought. "We're left holding the bag, guys."

The entire table swung around to look at Rey Rey.

"As Marg said, even with insurance, the insurance company could come after us for any financial problems the club experiences. Marg's right: we should find out the details of Kendrick's forty years in Northern Ontario. Now we have Everet and his missing forty years. Anybody have any ideas about how to go about this?"

There was no response. Rey Rey, the recently retired undertaker, answered his own question. "Perhaps we look at death records for the past forty years. Maybe he murdered someone."

Forest replied, "If that were the case, he wouldn't be here serving drinks. He'd be serving time. Why don't we just ask him to fill out an employment application and a list of references?"

"Rather late for that now, don't you think?" said Gail. "If he's hiding something, he certainly wouldn't put it on an employment application form. His knickers would be in a knot and he'd be doubly suspicious about why we're asking. Forget it. That's not the way to go."

Dakari spoke. "We should go on the internet and find out all references to the two of them. If they've done something bad, it'll show up. At least, that's what I hear."

There was complete silence around the table.

"What did I say, guys? Why the blank faces? Surely one of us knows how to use the internet."

He glanced around the table. "Stupid suggestion. Does anybody have a computer? None of us know how to make the internet work, do we?"

Gail had been silent until now. "I know a little about how to use a computer and I know how to access the internet to send emails. That's the extent of my knowledge. I hate computers and avoid them whenever I can. Count me out on this one."

"So," Dakari continued, "the answer is no."

Forest spoke up. "We have to go where Kendrick was. And Everet. We have to talk to the people they were involved with. Their friends and neighbours, even their business associates."

Instead of the recent disappointed looks, everyone's face lit up.

"Oh, I like that," said Gail, images of Sherlock Holmes and Dr. Watson dancing in her head. The same type of images must have flashed in the other heads, prompting many smiles. She continued.

"Do you think we're onto something? Maybe it's like the Enwright sisters, poisoning poor Finley. Remember, none of us even suspected them."

Memories of the murder of two members of the club last year flooded their brains. The excitement of finding out that two of the

Blue Duck Social Club members poisoned another member was fresh in their minds. Maybe this was a repeat. No one felt the least bit guilty about referring to it or even dwelling on it. Nobody liked Finley.

"I'm with that. It makes sense." said Dakari. "When do we start?" In his mind, he was already packed and ready to go.

"Whoa, not so fast, people," said Forest. "Let's plan this out. We've got plenty of time."

"No, we don't, Forest," Gail retorted. "Just ask the citizens of Pompeii, who got out of bed late. They didn't have any time before they were smothered. Maybe Kendrick is plotting right now. He could be gone tonight, for all we know. With our money."

Forest didn't want to relinquish his thought. "It never happens that fast. I know firsthand." In a very brief moment of levity, he continued, "It took them five years to find out I was a drunk before they let me go." Gail's mouth dropped.

The excitement of investigating generated ideas from everyone. A planned and logical approach was forgotten. Rey Rey asked, "Who do you think we should talk to? Do we start with the Chief of Police in some town in Northern Ontario?"

Gail looked puzzled. "Can you actually do that? Can you just walk in from the street and ask if Kendrick Overland is a criminal?"

Forest harrumphed and spoke up. "In my job, I had to review employment applications. All I had to do was go to the police station and ask for information on the applicant. They always gave it to me. We can do the same."

"What about his customers? How do we even find them?" asked Gail.

Dakari, smiling broadly, volunteered his opinion. "We'll walk around town and talk to anyone wearing a bathing suit. It's simple."

A frown appeared on Forest's face immediately. "I don't think that's realistic, Dakari. It's now September. No one wears a bathing suit at this time of the year."

The other people looked at Forest in disbelief. Forest responded, "I think I'm right. Why are you looking at me like that?"

Gail nudged his arm. "Let it go, Forest. Right now, what's important is who is going to organize the trip?"

Dakari had a thought. "I think we should put Rey Rey in charge. He's got lots of experience organizing events. How many funerals have you handled, Rey Rey?"

Rey Rey's chest pumped up. "I can do that. Give me a day and let's meet at the funeral home. Nobody can overhear us. Kendrick shouldn't know what we're up to, right? Where is Kendrick, anyway? Why hasn't he returned?"

The question was ignored, lost in the excitement of a new venture for the retired group. They had a purpose and an action plan. Dakari's enquiring mind thought otherwise, but it was too soon to rain on the parade.

The group moved towards the exit, talking and gesticulating excitedly. The doors opened to bright sunlight, highlighting a jungle of political signs near the entrance. Forest ignored them and turned his face to the warmth.

"Hey guys, it's an omen, a good luck omen. I've got this gut feeling that we're going to be successful," said Forest.

Dakari kept his silence, wondering what criteria Forest, the forty-year receivables manager, would define as success. Dakari was sure it was nowhere near his own definition. Even if they knew, he thought, what was their plan to reach it?

Chapter 4

The Blue Duck group left at five-thirty, leaving nothing but empty chairs. At six o'clock, the evening manager showed up.

"Slow day, Kendrick?" he asked, watching Kendrick pick up the remnants of the afternoon service.

"Must be a record day, Ernie. It never stopped, nor did I."

Ernie silently laughed. It was Kendrick's standard reply, and from the scarce number of unwashed glasses in the dishwasher, he knew it was bullshit. He turned away and accurately mouthed Kendrick's next comment. "I'm bushed Ernie. I can hardly wait to get home and put the old legs up for a rest."

Kendrick slowly made his way to the front door and exited to his van. Ernie moved to see the van through the front window, a show he enjoyed every night. Kendrick turned the ignition key; the engine backfired, and an enormous cloud of blue exhaust spewed from the tailpipe, partially obscuring the big-bosomed, bikini-clad starlet displayed on each side of the van. She was young at one time but had aged along with Kendrick, her painted image showing a cobweb of weather induced cracks.

The ten-minute drive to his condo allowed time to consider the questions about his absence from Port Detour. Why were his classmates curious about why he left Port Detour and what he had done for the last forty years? What did they know? His best friend

Forest was one of the group. Maybe he would tell him. He punched in Forest's cell number.

"Hi Kendrick," the familiar voice answered. "Are you all finished for the day?"

"Yeah, I'm on my way home. I'm ready to put my feet up, Forest. It sure was a busy day. I hope that good-looking blond down the hall leaves me alone. She came on to me this morning, you know."

"No, I didn't know, Kendrick. Still got the touch, eh?"

Kendrick could almost feel the envy in Forest's voice, coming from a man who had spent forty years with the same company and the same woman, That was until last year, when in a moment of remorse for a boring life, he left his wife and moved in with Gail, a high school classmate.

Forest continued. "But I'm glad you called. When you asked me to do the morning setup, I never thought I'd be picking up garbage and empty bottles and washing the floor for two hours.The place was a mess when I got there at nine this morning. Ernie didn't do his job last night. I'm right, aren't I? It wasn't you. It was Ernie. Maybe you should fire him."

"No need to be that drastic, Ernie. I'll talk to him."

"Oh yes, there's something else I forgot. You had a visitor this morning. What a coincidence. Marg also ran into him downtown. She told us this afternoon."

There was silence on the other end. "Kendrick, are you there?" Forest asked.

"Sorry Forest, that was me last night. Ernie had a family problem, so I worked the evening shift. Man, was it busy. I got run off my feet. What's this about a visitor? Was it the drag queen of Port Detour?"

Forest's answer was hesitant and serious. "No, I didn't know we had one in town." There was a pause. "You're pulling my leg, right?"

"I'd never do that to you, Forest. If it wasn't Candy Cane, who was it?"

"This well-dressed gentleman showed up. It was your older brother, Everet. He said he ran into Marg downtown and found out you were working at the Blue Duck. He introduced himself, asked about you, and wondered if he could get your address. Apparently, the one he had was out of date and you hadn't let him know where you were now living. I gave him your address. I kind of remember him. It was so long ago. And he must be older than us, say, by three or four years?"

"Yes, he's older, Forest. I told you that this afternoon."

"It's strange Kendrick, he didn't appear to be anything like you described. You said he screwed you, but this guy was nice. He had his son with him, about twenty-five or thirty, I'd guess. The kid was a charmer. Very polite with movie star looks. Are you sure we're talking about the same guy?"

Kendrick's speed slowed to a crawl. He refocussed just in time to see the semi-circle driveway of his new condo. Kendrick turned in and drove the labouring beast into the No-Parking zone directly across from the entrance doors.

"Believe me Forest, I've only got one brother, and he's a piece of work. Gotta go, Forest. The President of the condo is waving to me. He must want my opinion. Happens all the time."

An elderly gentleman exited the revolving doors of the condo lobby, looked straight ahead, and stopped as soon as his running shoes hit the sidewalk. He looked over at the large cube van, focussing on the young starlet displayed on both sides. Kendrick swiftly exited the van, walked towards the building and reached the lobby doors when Mr. Swartz yelled out, "Love that van, Kendrick," casting an admiring eye at the starlet's principal assets.

"You should drop in, Mr. Swarts. I've got the perfect bathing suit for your wife. You'd be a hero."

"Too old, Kendrick. Maybe I could get one for my mistress. She's only sixty-eight, you know. Still has a great body," he cackled, as he ambled by. He continued looking at the woman's body image on the van and seemed to connect some dots. His head rotated to Kendrick.

"Why haven't you got a lady? You can still get it up, right?"

Kendrick was about to answer the question when he thought of the five ex-wives and the trouble they had caused. Kendrick let it pass, pressed his security card on the sensor, and took the elevator to his condo on the fourth floor. He was tired. It wasn't the work at the tavern that caused it. No, he reflected, it was Everet's reappearance. Mental strain does that to a person. Tonight, it was going to be a Coors Lite and a frozen pizza for supper. He stripped and threw his clothes on the bedroom floor, put on his old paisley dressing gown, and returned to the kitchen. At eight-thirty the pizza was all gone, the television news was getting repetitious, and he was on his second beer and nodding off in the Lazy-Boy. That's when he heard the voice.

"Hey Kendrick, it's me."

The knock on the door startled him. He didn't move for a few seconds. The knocking continued but made little sense to him. If he could hear a knock on the door and a voice, why hadn't he heard the lobby intercom announcing a visitor? He rose from his Lazy-Boy, shoved the remains of the pizza and the empty Coors Lite to one side of the coffee table, and weakly called out, "Who is it?"

The knocks increased in intensity. A political canvasser? No, it coudn't be an outsider. It must be a fellow resident, no doubt the good-looking blond neighbour down the hall. That's why the intercom hadn't been used. The peep-hole provided a clear view of the hallway and the fishbowl lens took in a full body view of the person on the other side.

He could feel his heart rate jump, but it wasn't because of the blond with the big chest. It was Everet. Even after a ten-year gap, he easily recognized his older brother.

"I know you're in there, Kendrick. I saw your eye. Open the door," said the big voice on the other side.

"Go away, I'm not here," Kendrick replied in a much smaller voice.

"I've got all evening. It's your choice." Kendrick gave in and opened the door to an older version of himself. As Everet entered the condo, he thrust his right hand towards Kendrick in greeting and met his eyes directly. Kendrick didn't shake his hand.

"Nice to see you, bro. It's been a long time," said the older version.

The setting sun's rays cast a harsh, almost surrealistic light, directly on Everet, unfavourably sharpening the wrinkles on his tanned face. Both men were tall and trim, broad-shouldered, and had a wavy crop of light brown, partially grey hair. The difference was the clothes. Kendrick was in his housecoat. Everet was dressed like he had stepped right out of GQ, wearing a sand coloured suit, crisp white shirt and matching tie and puff. Even his Rolex looked like the real thing. He turned, grabbed the arm of a younger version of the Overland family and dragged him into view.

"This here is your nephew, Roland. Great addition to the family, don't you think?"

Kendrick didn't require any thinking. Nobody would mistake Roland for anything other than a relative of the two of them. Roland's perfect tan, white teeth and sparkling blue eyes made him noticeably attractive. His sandy coloured hair was thick and loosely combed back. But his most pronounced feature was the light blue/grey eyes rivetted on Kendrick. He wore a small gold ear-ring in his left ear and multi-coloured tattoos covered his hands and presumably well up his arms.

Kendrick made no motion to invite them in any further than the foyer. Everet glanced around, taking in the modern furnishings, the colourful abstracts on each wall and the two boldly patterned rugs in the living and dining areas. Rollie had no interest in the surroundings and spoke directly to his uncle.

"It's good to see you again, Uncle Kendrick," he said, in a firm and pleasant voice. "I remember you from the last time we met. It's been over ten years since Grandpa's funeral, hasn't it? Dad has told me many grand stories about the two of you growing up together. I feel I know you well."

Unlike most people Kendrick saw at the tavern, this young man was neatly dressed, well groomed and, as Kendrick realized out, his speech avoided the 'uhs' and 'likes' and 'y'know' used to ad nauseum by most other young people. This person could easily pass for a winner.

"I doubt that, Roland. Your father and I are as far apart as the two sides of the Grand Canyon. We've only seen each other twice in the past forty years." Kendrick's mind also added, silently, 'I never liked him, anyway'.

Everet ignored the non-invitation and ambled into the living and dining areas. The kid followed his father as Everet made a half-circuit of the room, looking around as if he was on an inspection tour. Kendrick stood still, waiting to hear why he was here.

"Do you own this, Kendrick? You were always a spender. Win the lottery?"

Everet was closer to the truth than he realized. For a moment, thoughts of the windfall filled Kendrick's memory cells. He had hooked up with Crystal almost immediately after arriving back in Port Detour, two years ago. She was a looker with an aspiration to have her own TV fashion show. She also mentioned a big bag of money from her last divorce. When Kendrick claimed he had his own radio fashion show in Northern Ontario, it was love at first sight. First sight didn't last long. Six months later, she announced, "Kendrick, you're nothing but a bullshitter and a liar. I just found out you never had a fashion show. I'll give you credit, you're smooth, but I wonder what other crap have you spouted? It's the end, Kendrick."

Kendrick had denied it all. "If somebody told you that, it's a monstrous lie. You know I was in the fashion industry with my shop for forty years. Everyone in Northern Ontario knew me. You're the one who's lying. Where's all this money you said you had when we married? I've paid for every expense since then."

"Kendrick, I've got more money than I could spend in my lifetime. But you said you had a ton of money. In fact, I remember your words – 'If money was like horseshit, I'd never get the stables clean' - or something like that. Why would I give you money?"

It was a good point, he thought. Remembering the stupidity of his comment yanked him back to the present.

Crystal had purchased a new condo unit, furnished it, and then announced it was all Kendrick's if she didn't have to set eyes on him for the rest of her life. Kendrick jumped at the offer.

"It's all mine, Everet. A lifetime of hard, honest work paid for it. By the way, what did you buy? Where is it?"

Everet stared at Kendrick for a fraction of a second before responding.

"I sold my place in the States for two mill and I'm looking for a country place just outside of Port Detour. Maybe you know of one, your must run in those circles."

He smiled faintly, but his eyes danced with pleasure at the one upmanship. He continued, "I wonder what Mom and Dad would think if they could see us now. Their two successful sons with money to burn. Do you ever think about it? "

"You didn't come here to reminisce, Everet. What do you want?"

Rollie, standing alongside his father, suddenly took an interest in the conversation, smiling slightly, and swung his gaze to Everet. Kendrick noticed the motion and thought Rollie might already know the answer.

"Well, well, it's Mr. Charm in person. I value family, bro. I just wanted to see you and renew our brotherly love. We're going to be a family again, you and me, plus I heard you got yourself another squeeze. You certainly run through them quickly. Isn't this number four?"

Kendrick, stupidly, in his mind, felt a need to explain. "No, Crystal was number five, but I just split with her. I'm on my own."

"Wow, that didn't take long. You've only been back two years. You work even faster than I do, Kendrick."

"And what about you?" Kendrick asked, wanting to change the subject. "You're no slouch in the love game. Three times married, right?"

Everet didn't react. Nor did Rollie.

"Yeah, I know more about you than you can imagine. For the past thirty years, every police force in North America has contacted me. They said they were only verifying your references and history, but some questions sounded like an investigation to me."

Everet continued to stare at him.

"From the questions, I figure you're a con artist. You must be successful. No one ever said you were arrested. Only one instance of violence. You got shot in the leg."

Rollie remained impassive and Everet completely ignored the remark. "Perhaps we could do some double dating now that I'm back. You and me, just like the good old times." His big laugh filled the condo.

"Everet, we never had good times together. You shafted me, or have you conveniently forgotten that? It nearly destroyed my life. You haven't got one moral bone in your body and I can't imagine that's changed."

Everet's look of hurt innocence was good enough to win an Oscar. He held his hand over his heart and frowned at Kendrick.

"I shafted you? You've gotta be kidding. Thanks to me, you were set on the straight and narrow. You hurt me to the quick, Kendrick." His hurt look quickly disappeared, to be replaced with a straight face, no emotion showing.

Rollie looked at his father. "Dad, you're off track. Tell uncle Kendrick about the opportunity."

"Oh yeah. Thanks Rollie. You want to know why the boy and I have moved back here? We're going to help this community, my hometown, and you." Kendrick quickly concluded Everet had a plan – no doubt an illegal one.

"I've got a lot to tell you, Kendrick. And now I've found something that's the golden goose. You remember the story, don't you? A guy has a goose that lays golden eggs. He doesn't have to do nothing. That's when I thought of you. You've spent all that time in the boondocks. Now you need a reward."

Kendrick had heard enough. Everet wasn't even as good at lying as he was. His emotions suppressed, he forced the words out in a normal voice. "I can hardly wait to hear about it, but right now it's past my bedtime. I have a heavy day tomorrow. It's time for you to leave."

"Yeah sure, I get it. Quite a surprise, us showing up, eh? I don't suppose you might have an extra room?" Kendrick's stare was the answer. "OK, OK, just asking," Everet responded.

"You know, we're family, after all. But I get it. We'll be in touch once we find a place to live. Are there any other condos for sale in this building?"

Kendrick continued to stare. Everet smiled, almost a leer, and said, "C'mon Rollie, let's leave uncle Kendrick for now." He turned and opened the door, pushed Rollie through it, and turned to face Kendrick. "We'll talk, bro. Good to see you." He winked as if we were sharing a conspiracy and added a parting comment.

"It's a golden goose for you and me. Let the money roll." His smile was glamorous, but he was still not believable. Or was he? What if he really had the golden goose?

But it was the young movie star who had the smarts and the manners. "See you, unc. It was so great seeing you again. I'm looking forward to hearing more about your experiences. From what Dad has told me, they sound fascinating. Have a great evening."

Kendrick closed the door quickly. They may change their mind. Even though the royal tour wasn't longer than ten minutes, Kendrick's teen age memories came rushing back, filling his mind and consciousness. And what experiences was Rollie talking about?

In his mind's eye, Everet's lack of support and his betrayal forty years ago had set a life course for Kendrick over which he had little control. Everything was Everet's fault – the eighteen months nightmare spent in a juvenile detention centre surfaced every day since then. Again, why was he back?

Growing up together provided Kendrick with a rare insight into his brother's personality. Everet was only concerned with himself, his mind a labyrinth of evil. Maybe Everet knew about the murder, the real reason Kendrick left Port Detour.

That got Kendrick thinking. What difference would another murder make?

Chapter 5

Kendrick drove the van as if in a trance. Behind him, the six cars in Port Detour's version of the morning rush hour beeped. Bicycles overtook him, but he hardly noticed. Thoughts of Everet hung heavy in his mind, like a storm cloud about to burst. It had been forty years. What and where had his brother been hiding all this time? What did Everet know about Kendrick?

He soon reached the parking lot of the Blue Duck, parked in the handicapped zone, and let himself into the tavern. As he entered, the smell of stale beer hit his nose, the result of no air conditioning for twelve hours. He quickly switched the air conditioning on, busied himself with cleaning up any remnants from yesterday, removed the washed glasses from the dishwasher and straightened all the tables and chairs. At noon, he was ready and unlocked the front doors. A surge of waiting bodies crossed the threshold and into the dark panelled room with its brightly lit bar and row of high bar stools lining the perimeter.

They all greeted Hendrick with a "Hi Kendrick," or "Afternoon, Kendrick."

For the first time in two years, Kendrick Overland, now drying glasses behind the bar, didn't greet them with a high five or a "Great to see you, my friend." His voice was subdued, and he replied with a "Hi."

Within an hour, most of the mis-matched chairs were occupied and each of the dark oak round tables displayed a collection of draft beer or glasses of white wine. Rey Rey and Marg were the last to arrive and joined their gang, sitting at a corner table in full view of the bar. Gail Alexander, Forest Green and Emile Bartlet acknowledged them with a nod, like old family members.

Rey Rey frowned, looked around the table and quietly asked, "What's with Kendrick?"

Forest Green harrumphed and felt it was his position to offer an opinion. "I don't think it's anything. You can't be upbeat all the time like Kendrick. Maybe he has a hangover." He sat back with a satisfied look on his face, his powers of observation no doubt apparent to all the other members. Nobody offered a different insight.

"I know," said Rey Rey. "Remember yesterday? He said he would tell us what he's done for the past forty years. It doesn't look like we're going to find out. He seems to be in a snit today. Marg, what did you say to him?"

"Me? Why me? All I said, and it was only to you, is that he's trouble. If he won't tell us, we can't do anything about it. Maybe we can discuss this further at the meeting."

Today, Tuesday, was the weekly meeting of the Club and the ritual was now well established–a drink upon arrival and the meeting at two o'clock. The '76 Class of Port Detour High were the founding members and Forest Green was the President. Two years ago, they bought the tavern when the long-time owner, Ducky Matte, had a heart attack. The purchase was controversial, the spouses unanimously criticizing the five hundred dollar individual investment and having to borrow the rest. The members were unanimous about the wisdom of the purchase.

"There is no way we can lose money," said Kendrick Overland at the time. "If it doesn't, I'll personally drink it back to success. Anyway, I've been a successful investor all my life and I know a good deal when I see one. This is a gold mine."

Marg quietly said to Rey Rey, "A successful investor who drives around in a broken down purple bus. That certainly invites confidence in his judgement. But I think it could be an excellent investment. I'm in." She wasn't alone.

Two years later, it was time to count the chickens and Forest Green couldn't wait for the meeting to start. Forty years working for Smith & Sons had not prepared him for the euphoria he was now experiencing. For the first time in his life, he had led a group of people to new heights. The tavern was a roaring success. Forest had been in charge of Accounts Receivable for Smith & Sons, and precision was his specialty. He was also the treasurer of the club, and had verified the accounts to his personal satisfaction.

It was only one forty-five, but he couldn't wait any longer. He stood up from his chair. "Let's get the meeting going," he shouted.

The volume of his high-pitched voice caused everyone, members and patrons alike, to stop talking and stare at the thin man in the short-sleeved shirt and the high water pants, his few strands of hair neatly combed across his nearly bald head.

"Another record month for the Blue Duck Tavern and its owners, the Blue Duck Social Club." His face now broke into a wide grin. "We have money in the bank and," he paused for effect, "we'll declare our first dividend at our meeting today."

The members looked at each other with smiles of disbelief. Their investment had paid off. The motion to declare a dividend was passed instantly.

It was now useless to bring up any other business. The news about the dividend was all anyone could talk about to the extent it displaced any thought of further business discussions.

Forest gave up trying to bring the meeting to order and moved to circulate among the members, basking in the glory like the owner of the prize winning hog at the Port Detour Fall Fair. The noise level was high, everyone trying to talk at once. Suddenly, around two o'clock, the front doors opened with a bang and a voice shouted out, "I'm back!" Many members held their drink in mid-motion, trying to understand who was back.

"Hi Forest, great to see you again," the newcomer shouted as he moved to Forest with a swagger and immediately put a bear hug on him. Everet wore a blue blazer, tan slacks and an open collared white shirt nearly obscured with three large gold chains. The facial features caught everybody's attention. Kendrick and the newcomer could easily be twins.

He released Forest from his hug, rotated to face the audience, his smile dazzling..

"I'm Everet Overland, and," he raised his arm and pointed at Kendrick, "this here's my brother. The best looker in the family."

Forest jumped in before Everet could keep the monologue going.

"Everyone, please welcome Everet Overland. Everet has been away from Port Detour for over forty years, but he's come back. Not only come back, he dropped in yesterday and asked if he can become a member of our club since he is also a graduate of Port Detour High."

Forest tried to continue with his introduction, but Everet moved in front of him.

"It's great to be back in Port Detour. I've been away much too long. There are so many fond memories of growing up here. But I have to admit, I made a mistake."

He paused and looked around the room, making eye contact with as many people as possible. There was a longer pause when he got to Marg or Gail or the other recently recruited female members, Gert and Lydia.

His face brightened up, and he almost shouted, "I should never have left." Everyone clapped, with one exception. Marg didn't move a muscle.

"Hey barkeep," Everet shouted, pointing at Kendrick standing behind the bar, "how about a beer for a thirsty relative?" Kendrick didn't acknowledge the demand other than to slowly turn towards the draft taps and even more slowly pour a draft of beer. He set it on the bar for Everet to pick up. Everet grabbed his beer and waded into the assembled crowd like a politician on a mission.

"Hi there. It's a real pleasure meeting you. What's your name?"

Within ten minutes, he had circulated the room and left smiles on everyone's face, except for Marg O'Toole. She, Gail, Forest and Emile stood chatting when he arrived. He grabbed Marg's hand and said, "Hi, good-looking lady. What's your name?"

She shook her head and slowly said, "I'll have my hand back, please." She took a step back and announced, "My name's Marg. Surely you remember, don't you?"

He paused, inspected Marg's face, and let his eyes roam down her body. "There's something about you I can't place. It must have been a high school event, but remember, I was ahead of you by at least three years."

Marg raised her brows. "Oh, I remember, Everet. I'm surprised you don't."

"I really don't, Marg. Maybe we were at a convention in Toronto and were blasted. Could that be it?"

"Not likely," she said, in the flat tone of an experienced lawyer cross-examining a witness. "Our paths may have crossed in the courthouse. I was a criminal defence lawyer in Toronto for many nasty people over the years. What kind of trouble were you in?"

Everet broke out in a laugh. "That's a good one, Marg. I've lived in the US for years, so it couldn't have been in Toronto. Anyway, I now remember where. You were a cheerleader, right? I used to go out with one of you, Marianne something. You were one good looking group of girls. Really hot. Oops, can't say that anymore." His laugh could be heard throughout the room.

"Yeah, that's it." He looked at her more closely, as if inspecting a side of beef, the added, "You were a couple of years ahead of me, right?"

Marg ignored the comment, and the conversation continued on without her participation. She turned away from Everet to look at the brightly lit bar. A frown appeared and for a moment she appeared to be detached from the group, as if in her own world. Gail looked at her friend and quietly asked, "What's the matter, Marg? Are you feeling OK?"

She answered in a low tone. "It's just something that happened a long time ago, Gail. I can't change it. Kendrick, and now Everet, are lying through their teeth. I can detect a lie from a hundred metres, Gail. They both remember the incident. Here's a thought. If they will lie about that, what else are they covering up?"

Marg's mind was confused. Did she want everything revealed, or was it better hidden? Her life had been affected by the experience, to the extent she trusted no one. She kept it buried.

"Anything you want to tell me, Marg? Would that make you feel better?"

"It wouldn't change what happened, Gail, but it's best to leave sleeping dogs lie. For now." After a pause, she added, "Mark my words, Gail, they'll pay for what they did. I just haven't figured out how."

Gail rejoined the conversation and asked, "So what's up, Everet? Why are you back?"

"I'm just a Port Detour hometown boy at heart, Gail. I've been in the States all my working life, but it's time to get out of that cesspool. Also, I've got a great business opportunity right here, in good old PT. Got my son to help me. The kid needs something to do besides chase women."

"And what did you do in the States, Everet?"

"It's been a dream. I saw how to make big time money in real estate. I made a fortune. It's a great place to make money, but you don't really want to be there now, Trump and all that crap."

As if he wanted to cut off any further discussion, he turned to face Emile Bartlet, who had been chatting with Marg, and introduced himself.

"And what's your claim to fame, Emile? Lawyer, maybe?"

"Police Chief, Everet. You know, the guy who catches the bad ones."

"Really. We've got all kinds in the club, haven't we, Emile? I bet you got stories to tell up the wazoo." He took a gulp of his beer and shifted his gaze, looking directly over Emile's shoulder. "Oh, I think I see someone I might have known. Excuse me."

Marg followed Everet's departure and immediately he was out of earshot, she turned to Emile and said, "Well that was a quick exit. One thing he said about you is intriguing. I bet you know more about everyone here than their own mothers. What's the scoop on Everet?"

"Marg, I'm retired, so I guess the secrecy thing doesn't apply to me anymore. Here's what I know."

Marg leaned in closer. As far as she knew, it was the first time a police authority had shared info with a defence lawyer.

"Over the years, we got dozens of enquiries from other police forces in Canada and the US, all having to do with security and fraud. But more importantly, I know why he left Port Detour. When Everet was nineteen years old, we were hard on his heels for convenience store break-ins. It was only a matter of time before the evidence confirmed it. He stupidly sold cartons of cigarettes from the trunk of his car to anyone who showed up, including a plain-clothes officer. He left town for parts unknown before we could charge him. Too late now."

Marg was surprised by her response. It was as if living in Port Detour removed any constraints on her mind, especially trust. In Port Detour, you got what you saw, no pretence, no posturing. "Ooh, I love it. What have you got on me? Want to tell me sometime?"

Emile stammered something unintelligible and moved to sit down at their table. Marg overcame her out-of-body reaction and joined him. Without saying a word, they both followed Everet's journey around the crowd. Within minutes, he took a seat at the next table with Gert and Lydia. Lydia said little, but Everet's conversation with Gert was easily heard. Everett was in full-on voice volume and his laugh shook the room.

"So, Gert, what's a beautiful woman like you done since we were last in school? Let me guess. Modelling? Mayor?" Kendrick, in the process of serving the two women, almost spilled the glass of beer he set down in front of her.

"I'm a widow, Everet."

"What a coincidence. So am I, Gert. It's a lonely life, isn't it?"

There was no preliminary conversation, just a direct approach. Everet's one way conversation carried on for a few minutes, until he rose from his chair, looked around at the other tables, and then back to Gert. "Can I call you?" he asked.

She looked close to crying. "I'd love that, Everet." Everet made a slight bow, turned and headed straight for his next single female destination.

The excitement of finding out how great their investment was and the probability of a dividend was grand news, but it was only three o'clock and once a weekly routine has been started, it's hard to break. It wasn't time to leave. As always, the beer was as refreshing as the conversation. Home couldn't compete with that.

The groups gradually reassembled in the same combination as before the meeting started. The only topic, other than the dividend on their wise investment, was Evere

Marg and Emile continued to watch Everet's progress around the room. It didn't take him long to reach the end of his journey, making quick jokes at each table and leaving compliments in his wake. The smiles proved everyone loved him. He carried his near empty beer glass across the room to the table where Marg, Gail, Forest, Dakari and Rey Rey had gathered..

"Got room here?" he asked in a loud voice, a big smile on his face. He sat down, not waiting for an invitation.

Kendrick appeared with refills for the group. "Do you want another draft, Everet?"

"Naw, I've had enough. Water would be great. Some Perrier with one ice cube and a twist of lemon. Forget the swizzle stick." He swung his gaze to his table mates as if expecting looks of congratulation on his wise choice. Kendrick returned quickly and set the Perrier in front of Everet. He just stood there awkwardly and then mumbled something about how slow it was today.

"Do you mind if I join you? It's like old times."

"For sure, Kendrick," said Marg. "Pull up a chair." He said nothing when he sat down and stared intently at Marg, who did not turn away.

Marg continued. "Anyway, Kendrick, let's get on a subject close to your heart." She turned and faced Everet. "Let's have our newest member, your brother, tell us about his history. Everet, have you led as mysterious a life as Kendrick?" she asked him.

"Nothing mysterious about me, guys. My life's an open book. But it could sound like a fairy tale. I told some of you I got lucky in real estate, but that wasn't my real occupation. Who wants to guess?"

Kendrick spoke up first. "Something illegal, right? That's why you're back in Canada." Everyone looked at him and Gail remarked, "That's not funny, Kendrick." But the dam had broken, and the answers shot out. Fireman, antique dealer, car salesman, and train engineer.

With each answer, he said no and laughed even louder. "Give up. You'll never guess."

He looked around at the group for thirty seconds, then looked at his watch as if to make sure the pause maximized the expectation.

Marg was used to being conned. The criminal clients she represented were some of the best liars in the world. Few of them were what they appeared to be. They really wanted people to believe they were another person, a person who was innocent and trustworthy. In other words, a confidence artist. She recognized talent when she saw it. Everet was one of the best.

"I'm a clown."

Everybody starred at him. Kendrick perked up and announced, "Perfect role for you, Everet. Required little training, did it?"

Chapter 6

For a moment, there was complete silence around the table, a tableau frozen in time. The swish of the overhead fans could be clearly heard. Each of the five people had open mouths and frowns. Was this a game? Whoever heard of this?

Finally, Gail spoke up. "You've got to be kidding." There was a collective sigh of relief, as if the word dam had been broken and the words were now flowing. "Yeah, Everet," said Dakari, "Did you say clown or down?"

"Clown, Dakari. Clown as in funny. It's true. I'm not only a clown, but I teach people how to be a clown. I'm good at it and I have assignments all around the world."

Marg squinted her eyes and cocked her head in disbelief. "That's bullshit, Everet. Get real."

Forest Green wanted to believe it. For a man whose highest ambition was to be a corporate manager, the idea of letting go your inhibitions ranked right up there with free love.

Everet looked around the table. Everyone had put their drink down and leaned forward as if Everet was going to let them into a secret world. Satisfied with the attention, he suddenly stood up, reached into his pants pocket, brought out a red bulb nose, put it on, messed up his hair and danced over to Dakari to remove his kufi hat and put it on his head.

He swept his arm around the table and said, "Believe me now?"

Every head at the table bobbed up and down. Forest was now a genuine believer.

"Have you done this for the past forty years, Everet?" asked Forest.

"Almost, Forest, but it's my hobby. After leaving Port Detour, I found the most worthwhile thing I could do was help other people. First, I studied to be a financial advisor and for the past forty years, I've advised clients how to invest wisely. But it's a younger person's game now, so I've reduced the number of clients I advise. Ten years ago, I got into real estate. That's where I made a fortune."

Marg leaned back from the table, wineglass in hand. She had to smile. At least it explained Everet's fashionable mode of dress. In her mind, she didn't believe a word of it. Why would Everet concoct such an elaborate life-story? It had to be a diversion. What was he really hiding?

"That's the most bizarre story I've heard in a long time. Nothing but bullshit."

He ignored her. "That's not all, folks. I found another part-time job, even better than clowning." He took the red bulb nose off and carefully smoothed his hair.

Forest, Gail and Rey Rey had one job their whole life. Whoever heard of having three jobs and a hobby. Forest knew first-hand. He had trouble handling one job and his birdhouse building hobby. Everet must be a genius, he decided.

"Go on, tell us," said Gail impatiently.

"For over ten years, I was a freelance cruise ship social director. Every four months of the year, I sailed the seven seas and made sure every passenger was having a good time. I had a ball, and so did the passengers. Especially the single ones." He winked suggestively.

Emile was intrigued. Maybe it explained the frequent requests he received asking about Everet.

"So, Everet, did you have to get security clearance for the cruise line and the securities firms?"

"Ahh, always the copper, Emile. Yeah, that was a hassle. For every assignment, I had to renew my security clearance. I visited nearly every large port in the world and my passport is stamped so many times it looks like a Walmart coupon book."

Kendrick was silent, taking it all in with no reaction, until he couldn't contain himself.

"It must have been quite the life, on board. Any rich widows or divorces looking for a husband?" His face could barely disguise the smirk. "Quite a combination. Rich women and an investment advisor."

Everet gave him a quick non-smiling glance and continued. "The cruise ship assignments were the most fun. There was always something happening. Like the time a guy was thrown out of a woman's stateroom, completely nude. He couldn't get back into either his or her stateroom and ended up having to go to the purser's office to get a key."

The storytelling went on for an hour and the five original tablemates now had the company of at least six others who were attracted by the laughing. Everet had won them over, telling tale after tale. Even Marg, the big city lawyer, laughed at a few of them.

After the last story, she turned to Gail who was seated next to her and in a low voice, said, "Makes you wonder, doesn't it? It's hard to separate the truth from the bullshit."

She then turned to Kendrick, and in a loud voice, said, "Kendrick, it certainly looks like you and Everet have the same personalities. Are you sure you're not twins?"

Kendrick quickly responded with a shake of his head, "No way we're alike."

Everet took a sip of his Perrier and faced Kendrick. "But enough of me. What about my kid brother? Even I don't know what he's been up to these past forty years."

"Yes Kendrick, it's your turn," Gail said, her voice raised in anticipation. "We didn't hear the rest of your story yesterday. You told us you moved to Northern Ontario. Sudbury I think. Were you really there for forty years?"

"Yeah, just like Moses. Forty years in the desert. You want to know what I did up in Northern Ontario? Let me tell you."

He looked around the table and, satisfied that everyone was paying attention, began his story.

"Even up north, I still couldn't get a job for love or money. So I had this brilliant idea. I convinced a used car dealer to sell me a cube van on credit and I started a swim suit business. The van was my travelling store. It wasn't just a fresh start; it was a last resort."

Marg reacted in her logical way. "A swim suit business in Northern Ontario? You'd have more success selling manure to a farmer. Where did that idea come from?"

"Hey, I was young. A great way to meet women, wouldn't you say?"

She laughed a bit. "Only if you're naïve. How did it work out?"

"It was great, Marg. I was young, good looking, and had a great body. The women flocked to me when I pulled into town." He paused and grimaced. "The older women."

Everyone laughed and Marg added, "Serves you right, you old lecher. So, you were a success?"

"I worked my ass off, but since I travelled a lot, I had few friends. My consolation prize was to get married. Four times. But I rescued a few assets and now have a great nest egg."

"Kind of boring, Kendrick. I'll ask again. Are you sure you're not something else, like your brother?"

"No Marg, that's it. Just a plain and simple guy."

"But that's not the end of the story, is it, Kendrick? Why did you come back? No skeletons in the closet we should know about? Anything dead and buried before you left? Something forgotten after so many years?"

Everet was watching his brother intently. "Yeah, Kendrick, we know why I left. What about coming back? Are you sure you're telling us everything?"

Rey Rey, Marg, Emile, Gail and Dakari swung their gaze to Kendrick and noticed a brief flicker of concern in his widened eyes and a quick opening of his mouth.

"I told you what happened. That's it. There wasn't any drama. Only a kid wanting a job, that's all. That's why I left. Anyway, if there was some other reason, it would travel around Port Detour faster than a fart in a windstorm."

"And?" Marg asked.

Kendrick knew exactly what she was after. "And I came back because it was time to retire."

Emile leaned over to Marg, who was sitting next to him, and whispered, "He's smooth, and glib. How about you and I look at some old police files, Marg? Nothing happens in a small town which isn't recorded." Marg kept looking at Kendrick and nodded in agreement.

Kendrick looked over to the bar area and saw the evening sun streaming in, lighting up the glasses hanging down from the rack in the ceiling. He got up from his seat. "Back to work. I got some cleanup to do."

Kendrick's action seemed contagious. The group got up as if one, downed the remains of their drinks while standing, and headed to the front door. Some of them revisited Everet's exploits to each other with a fond laugh. Marg and Dakari were the only ones to openly question the stories.

Emile joined up with Marg and said, "There's something about both brothers that sounds loose, don't you agree?" Marg nodded, "Uh huh," in a knowing manner, "but how can we find out?"

Emile, without a word, made a 'come with me' head motion for her to follow him. He led her to his car, held the passenger door open and, once in place in the driver's seat, pointed it towards the road.

"Where to are you spiriting me away, Sir Gallant?"

Emile, married for thirty-five years and a widower for the last two, turned red in the face and hesitated, in search of a reply. "We're on the way to the police station, Marg." He briefly faced her, smiled and said. "So don't get any ideas."

He chuckled as if this was the funniest retort possible and added, "I may be retired, but that doesn't limit my access to all the police records, Marg. If there's something there about either man, we'll find it." Within five minutes, they were at the Port Detour Police Service building.

"I like the way you think, Emile. Where were you when I was looking for a man?"

Marg and Emile, when they walked through the front door of the Blue Duck, didn't notice another hookup. Everet made a point of hanging back, joining up with Kendrick as he came to lock the front door.

"What do you want?" Kendrick asked, frowning at his older brother.

"Remember, I said I had a golden goose? We can share in this one. You deserve it, considering you spent all those years wandering around the wilderness. How about I come over to your place around eight tonight and you can get the entire story?"

"Not if it's a repeat of forty years ago," said Kendrick.

"Nothing like that, bro. This is for real. And I need your help for it to work."

"How much real is it, Everet? One hundred grand? That would be real if it were all for me."

Everet's eyes lit up. He smiled, and he placed his hand on Kendrick's arm. "You'll be surprised, Kendrick, really surprised. See you at eight?"

The mention of one hundred grand made it a persuasive offer. Kendrick had a complete change of attitude. "Yeah, sure. See you at eight."

Chapter 7

The Port Detour Police Service building was completely unremarkable; it could have easily been mistaken for a local Walmart. Cement block and low-lying, it must have taken genuine effort for the architect to design something so out of keeping with the town's natural beauty.

Emile parked his car next to the side entrance, moved around the car and opened the door for Marg. Without a word, he led the way through the unlocked door and greeted the officer at the desk just inside the door.

"Hi Wayne, I'm here to check on something. Got a spare office?"

Wayne didn't act surprised nor make any attempt to ask why Emile was there. Emile may have been retired, but the Chief would always be the Chief to him. He got up and led the way down the long grey corridor and ushered them into a room with a desk, two chairs and a computer screen.

"Make yourself at home, Chief. The password is the same as when you left. If you need anything else, just call. I'm going down the hall to the records room."

They both pulled out a chair and Emile pulled the computer screen and keyboard closer so that both of them could see. There were no distractions in the room and whoever managed the decorating had been consistent. The grey colour of the hall carried on into the interview room walls with the added accent of black plastic chairs and a stainless steel table top.

"As I think back, Marg, we received an unusual number of calls about Everet Overland. I never thought much of it at the time since he was just a name to me. Let's see what all the fuss was about."

He tapped in Everet's name and a long list of enquires appeared on the screen. There was a heading and the source of the enquiry. When the heading was clicked, it brought up a summary of the enquiry. Interestingly, nearly all the enquiries were prompted by complaints from US citizens. A few were from security agencies and police forces, but these were in the minority. There was no information about what happened after the enquiry.

"Well, Marg, nothing very concerning other than the volume. I'll acknowledge one thing, though. What's the old saying? Where's there's smoke, there's fire? The problem is we don't have sufficient info about any of the enquiries to arrive at any conclusion. We'd have to talk to the source of the enquiry, and mabe the complainant, to find out what really went on."

"Sounds like a road trip to me, Emile. Are you up to it?"

His mind wrestled with the question, and he finally asked, "Are you blowing this out of proportion, Marg? There are no warrants for his arrest. It doesn't look like he's being pursued for bad debts. What do you expect to find?"

"Emile, he denied knowing me when I asked. There is no way he doesn't remember me, given what happened over forty years ago. Even today, I can't talk about it. It's that painful. But here's my take. Given that Everet says he doesn't remember me and given the volume of enquiries from law enforcement units in the US, there's something about the man we should know. I don't have any idea how it would affect us, but Forest has let this man into our club and, whether we like it, we're now associated with him and whatever he's been involved in over the past forty years."

"You could very well be right, Marg. Now that I think about it, my reputation is on the line here. Imagine the headlines–'Former Police Chief Emile Bartlet is buddy with terrorist and bank robber, Evert Overland'. Yeah, maybe a trip south of the border is the next step. I'm game."

Marg put her hand on Emile's arm, smiled, and looked him straight in the eye, "There's something else, Emile".

Emile had conducted many interrogations of criminals and suspects and it was quite unusual for someone to want to provide to additional information, at least voluntarily. Also, when the words 'something else' were said, it wasn't usually insignificant. Since he didn't have any idea what the 'else' could be, he sat and waited for Marg to tell him, with no prompting on his part.

She brushed back some loose strands of hair, sat more upright, and set her hands on the table.

"Emile, you remember when Kendrick arrived back on the scene two years ago? His reaction to meeting me was the same as his brother's. He claimed he couldn't remember me. Why? And why would they both leave Port Detour at nearly the same time?"

Emile was now in cop mode. Unanswered questions in mysterious situations always led to something outside the law.

"Good questions, Marg. Their leaving was well before my time, though. So I can only do two things. I can surmise or speculate or," he paused, knowing Marg would die to hear what it was, "I can check the police records around the time of their departures. Luckily, the Port Detour Police Service spent the money to digitize all the records in their files. Searching for info is child's play."

Marg thought differently. She had revealed to Emile only last week that she was a computer nerd. If anything could go wrong with her computer, it did. Her firm had offered to assign a junior person to provide computer support for her. She had gladly accepted the offer. Emile now enjoyed the fun of seeing Marg impetuously tapping her left foot and drumming the desk with her fingers, unable to offer any advice on how to search for what she wanted.

"Well, get on with it, Emile. What are you waiting for?" She looked at the computer screen as if she could will it into life. "Marg, you're one impetuous lady. I love it." He pushed the mouse around the surface and a search screen came up asking questions about what he wanted to see.

Marg couldn't wait. "Try the years when they both left, Emile." Emile dutifully entered the year 1976 and a long stream of police reports appeared. He typed in some filter words to remove any incidents about burglary, domestic violence, and other unrelated classifications. The remaining incidents couldn't have numbered over thirty. Two stood out.

"That's it, Emile," said Marg, pointing to the screen. "Bring up the details."

The first report provided details about a young man named Everet Overland selling stolen goods to undercover officers. They arrested him but he never made his court appearance. The report said that the amount of the theft was so small no one tried to find out where Everet was and the outstanding warrant remained in effect.

"Emile, is that warrant still good after forty years.?"

"No Marg. It's dead. Everet isn't wanted for anything."

Marg pointed to the second incident. It was interesting because of the names–Brown and Overland.

Emile called up the report, dated 1976. Police were called to the Good Fortune Bar and Grill on the outskirts of town at four in the afternoon. There had been an altercation between two young men, Kendrick Overland, and another similarly aged young man called Bart Brown. A fight had taken place in the parking lot and Bart was found unconscious, lying in a large pool of blood. He was taken to hospital with lacerations on his face, a severe cut on his head, and a suspected concussion.

"Is that all, Emile? Was anyone arrested?"

"No Marg. That's the end of the report, except for a note two months later saying that Kendrick was nowhere to be found and the incident was dropped when Bart didn't press charges."

The light went on even before she had read the last paragraph.

"That's it, Emile. I know why Kendrick left town. He believed he killed Brown. Kendrick was a big powerful guy, and the report has Brown at only one hundred and thirty pounds."

"You know, Marg, I think you're right. Kendrick already had a theft conviction and served time in a prison. Another offence and he'd be locked up for years."

"Could I ask you a favour, Emile? Can we keep this between ourselves? There's no need to let the others know this, and it might be of help if we ever have to confront Kendrick about his reasons for leaving."

"Sure, Marg. No problem." He tucked the request away in his mind for now. But it raised a question of what this had to do with Marg and Kendrick.

Chapter 8

Kendrick heard the elevator bell ring when it reached his floor, along with a raise in his heartbeat. It was one of life's mysteries, he thought. Why do elevators ring when they reached their destination? Maybe it was to wake up any sleeping passengers.

Everet bounded out of the opening before the door had fully retracted and headed to Kendrick's door, his happy face on as he approached.

"Going to a disco tonight, Everet?" asked Kendrick in response to the garish colours decorating his brother. A bright red scarf was wrapped around his neck, the colour matching his loafers. In between, there was nothing but black and gold. A black t-shirt and black denims were the background for three large link faux gold chains jangling around his neck. Three diamond zircon rings on each hand made him look like Tony Soprano of the TV mob show. He did a rotating dance step just to make sure Kendrick saw the entire ensemble.

"Great to see you, bro," he said as he sauntered into the condo. The smell of the remnants of a frozen TV dinner lingered in the air and the kitchen counter displayed a few dirty utensils and one empty beer glass. "Dining in, I see," he commented and, like his first visit, made a grand tour around the open planned unit, inspecting various objects, artwork and furniture.

"Trying to determine how much they might fetch at the pawnshop?" Kendrick asked. There was no reaction. "You're not in the will, if that's what you're thinking."

"No, no. This is good stuff, Kendrick. You've got good taste. Well done."

Putting the last piece of fake art back in place, he casually sat down on the sofa, legs stretched out, one arm flung over the back. His chains jangled. The other hand moved to slick back his thick hair. He had a broad smile, but no conversation.

"Make yourself at home," said Kendrick. The sarcasm was completely lost on Everet, who by this time had slid off his loafers. Kendrick hoped he wasn't waiting for the butler to appear with drinks.

Suddenly, Everet sat upright and said, "Have a seat." The happy face was replaced with a frown and, as Kendrick sat down on the end of the sofa, Everet blurted out, "I've got a problem, bro, and you're the only one who can help."

"Join the club, so have I. What do you want, Everett? I thought you were going to explain your 'golden goose' get rich scheme."

"Kendrick, I'm going to level with you."

"I'd be disappointed if you didn't, Everet. What's prompted that thought?"

"I've moved back to Port Detour for two reasons. The first is Rollie. The kid has been nothing but trouble since his mother left over ten years ago. His judgement is shitty, and you should see his choice of friends. No, that's not right, you don't want to be near his friends. I always check the house after they visit, just so I to know what they've taken."

Kendrick didn't know where this was going.

"You were always the smart one in the family, Kendrick. I hear you've got one kid, not that you'd tell me, right?"

"I've got a girl. I was married three times, but no output. Probably lucky, considering how kids are today. I can't stand them. Anyway, I couldn't care less. The fourth marriage stuck. We were together for nearly fifteen years. Then Carol died, and I moved back to Port Detour with the kid."

He frowned. "Anyway, what does that have to do with you and me? You dumped your problems on me when we were kids, so excuse me if I don't want any more of your problems. You're on your own. Where's your wife in all this?"

"Linda left ten years ago. God knows why."

"Everet, over the years, I got a slew of calls from all kinds of law enforcement agencies in the US. I know what you did. Maybe your brief holidays in jail or your womanizing on board cruise ships or the police at the door affected her judgment. People are sometimes bothered by that sort of thing."

"What are you talking about?" His face took on a hurt look, along with a quick shake of his head. "What makes you think I was ever involved with stuff like that?"

"Everet, I'm not too old to remember you as a teenager. Back then, you were never at fault, always being unfairly blamed, so you claimed. I doubt you've changed. What I also remember is your smooth talk. You could have been the best salesman in the world, but I suspect you probably became the best con artist in the world."

Everet seemed entirely unfazed by the accusation. "And just how did you reach that conclusion? I've never been convicted of anything like that. All you got were calls about security, right? I had some high level confidential jobs. How does that make me a con artist?"

Kendrick let it go. It was too easy for Everet to deny it.

"I know a lot about you, too. You got all the brains and the mouth. And we both know you got sent away for the wrong crime. The Port Detour police never knew the half of what you did. But I did. I saw it firsthand. Right? It would be interesting to find out what cons you pulled off in the boondocks of Northern Ontario. Not much competition up there, I bet. Certainly not smart enough for a guy like you."

For a moment, Kendrick's face lit up like a sunlit gap in a passing cloud. Then reality set in. He was sure Everet, the con man, was up to something. He could play that game just as well.

"Anyway, what's the deal? What's the second reason you're back here?"

"Do you like money, Kendrick? Lots of money?"

Over the next ten minutes, Everet wove a tapestry of opportunity, no risk, and a huge payoff. One of the security companies he worked for in the US wanted to establish a super-secure private location in Canada. The company wanted to locate outside a major city and needed an agent to get a building site and do the legal side of the startup. Everet was known to them, was a Canadian and knew the security business. He was offered a million dollar finder's fee to both get land and set up the legal entity.

"So, why do you need me?" asked Kendrick. "You can do all that yourself."

"Well, not really, bro. I got problems."

"No way, Everet. You? That's a surprise. Your problems wouldn't be of the break the law kind, would they?"

"Don't be a smartass with your older brother, Kendrick. Of course they are. Are you interested in helping me or not? I'm willing to share the fee with you, if that makes any difference."

Kendrick tried to hide his surprise by standing up and walking over to the picture window and gazing out over the moonlit lake. His calmness only lasted for a few seconds. He turned and rapidly spouted the words, "Five hundred thousand? Of course I'm interested. Who do I have to kill?"

The words prompted a smug look on Everet's face, a half smile. "It hasn't come to that yet, but it's good to know you're available. Here's what I need. I found a site before I even came back. It's owned by the town, which is no big deal, and they have identified it as surplus to their needs. I'm sure they'll sell."

"So, what's the problem?"

Everet had obviously thought a lot about this. His answer was swift. "I have a record in Canada and some other pending shit. You don't have to know about those and it doesn't change the deal. You'd only be involved in the purchase."

"Everet, I don't have that kind of money. Anyway, I wouldn't trust you after what you did to me. I'd like to keep my millions intact."

"There you go again. I'm amazed you accumulated anything. You must be the most conservative guy I know. This deal has no risk. No risk, Kendrick. It doesn't matter, anyway. My client is putting up all the dough. You don't need to risk anything."

"So what's the problem, Mr. No Risk?"

"Because of my criminal record, I'd never be approved to own a company, much less a license to operate a security company. That's where you come in. You set up the legal entity and get all the permits. My client funds the company, your company purchases the property, flips it to them and you get the one million dollar finder's fee. Just to be clear, again, you share 50/50 with me. How's that sound for an easy buck?"

Everet stood up, a satisfied look on his face, and walked over to join Kendrick at the window. The calmness of the lake seemed to provide evidence of a satisfying agreement between the two.

He did a quick "Yes, I could get used to this, bro. Maybe we can live together. I'll pay cash for my share."

Kendrick followed his gaze out over the lake. "Ever hear of a deal killer, Everet? No way that's going to happen. Take me through it again."

The next half hour was a regurgitation by Everet and questions from Kendrick. Finally, Kendrick ran out of questions and concluded the discussion with, "Let me think about the deal. I've got my own problems to resolve. I'll sleep on it and let you know tomorrow."

Everet clapped Kendrick on the back. "What's to sleep on, Mr. Conservative? This is a dream come true. I know this is going to work, bro." He added, "You deserve it."

As if the deal was done and there was no more need to be friends, Everet said, "If that's it, talk to you in the morning."

He opened the door and left.

Kendrick tried to think positive. Five hundred thousand dollars positive. He had all night to decide, but he knew deep down he was going to accept. Money really talks, he reflected.

Chapter 9

The door had barely shut as Kendrick picked up his cell phone and hit a number on his speed dial list.

"Forest Green here," came the voice through the speaker. "Who is this, please?" Forest still hadn't figured out how to activate the setting that showed who was calling.

"Forest, it's Kendrick. I've got a decision to make, and I'd appreciate your thoughts. It's about Everet."

"My gosh, Kendrick, it's nearly ten o'clock. You caught me just as Gail and I were going to bed. What's so important at this time of night?"

Kendrick ignored the question. Forest would never understand the need for urgency. As far as Forest was concerned, things happened. One just sat and waited. Except for the Blue Duck Social Club, which was formed to combat the boredom of retirement. Forest had never reflected on what they had accomplished. What would be the advantage of that?

Kendrick continued. "You're a finance guy, right? My brother Everet wants me to be partners with him in a deal. But I'm not into that high finance stuff. I need to talk to an expert, like you." Whether Kendrick believed his own words, platitudes were always welcomed by the receiver.

Kendrick explained the deal as best he could. Forest said he understood and offered some comments for Kendrick to consider. After a few moments of listening to several phrases foreign to him, Kendrick interrupted Forest.

"Tell me what you think. Is it a good deal for me?" asked Kendrick.

"First, Kendrick, you gotta be comfortable with your partner. I'm impressed with Everet, so step number one is a go. As to the flow of money, he's right. It's not your money, so there's no risk for you. You and Everet will end up with a huge amount of money. If I were you, I'd go for it."

"That's what I thought, Forest. But Forest, there's an old saying, if it sounds too good to be true, it probably isn't true. I think there's a catch here. But thanks for the advice. I got to think some more about this. Here's another question. The company would be in my name as owner and there wouldn't be any problem getting government approval. But there's no legal agreement with Everet. What if I don't share the money with him?"

"That's a strange question. Why wouldn't you?"

"Maybe I get greedy, Forest. It's been known to happen."

"From the little I know about Everet, even though he's a nice guy, I imagine he would torture and kill you and then take the whole million." Forest chuckled internally at his new-found lighter view of life.

"Get serious, Forest. That doesn't sound like your way of thinking. What you're really saying is if I don't give him his share, I'd have big trouble on my hands."

"Yeah Kendrick. People have killed for less. Take the deal."

That's easy for him to say, thought Kendrick. Forest's knowledge of Everet was from his brief encounter with him at the Blue Duck. Kendrick thought back to all those enquiries over the years from people looking for his brother. And Everet had a mean streak, with little regard for people's feelings. Was Everet capable of killing to get what he thought was his? Kendrick knew Everet's entertaining tales of the last forty years were all bullshit. Despite his denial to the Blue Duck group, he knew deep down that he and Everet could be twins. Like Kendrick, Everet, no doubt, had learned the dark ways to make a living over the past forty years.

There was no need to share his innermost thoughts with Forest. The conversation had ended as far as Kendrick was concerned. "Goodnight Forest."

Forest was a lightweight, thought Kendrick. He thought well of everyone. He needed to talk to someone who was more had-nosed than Forest. Kendrick looked up Marg's number and called her. The hello and how are you niceties didn't take long. Marg sounded cautious and guarded, he thought. He again explained the deal Everet had proposed.

"Sounds too good to be true, Kendrick. Tread carefully. Just make sure you don't put any money into the deal. You know who Everet is. Can you imagine the people he's acting for?"

"Marg, I've got to let you know something. I'm broke. I need the money. Badly. My ex-wives are bleeding me dry."

"Kendrick, what a surprise. Are you actually telling me you're behind on your payments?" There was a slight pause, then, "You're in deep shit, aren't you?"

If Marg were present, she'd be looking at a man with drooping shoulders, a nervous tick and a grim face. "Yeah, I'm going to lose my condo unless I make this deal work."

"I'd say Everet's got you by the balls. You don't have a choice. Go ahead, blow your brains out." Marg quietly said, under her breath, 'loser.' She continued. "What do you want me to do?"

"Marg, you being a lawyer and all, you probably know how to set up a company and get all the proper licences and bank accounts, right?"

"Of course, Kendrick," she snapped. Kendrick either didn't detect the tone or ignored it.

"Could you do that for me? No need to tell anyone. We want to keep it as private as possible."

The answer was swift. "Sure Kendrick. That's easy to do. But I'm not practising anymore. It'll have to be an associate of mine who will do the work, under my guidance, of course. When do you need it?"

"I'll call you, Marg. Probably tomorrow or the next day. Goodnight."

Marg's comments crystalized the deal. He was going to charge ahead. There was no other choice.

A sense of satisfaction, even relief, overcame him. Unusual for him, he found a tumbler, poured a small amount of scotch whiskey from a long unused bottle and sat down on the sofa. The lights of Port Detour glowed in the distance. His life was looking a small bit better.

His small satisfaction was suddenly interrupted by a horrible thought. Maybe he shouldn't have hesitated when Everet approached him. Maybe the deal was gone.

He instantly picked up his phone, dialled Everet's number, and breathed a sigh of relief when Everet answered. Without even a greeting, he got to the point immediately.

"Everet, I've decided. There's no advantage waiting until tomorrow. I'm in."

"Great, Kendrick. I'll leave it up to you to organize the company and all that other crap. You got to be quick, though. This deal will not be around forever. Just to confirm, before we go any further, I found the deal and these are my connections. It's sixty percent for me and forty for you."

"Everet, that's not what you said earlier. It's fifty-fifty."

"No Kendrick, it's sixty - forty. You have a problem with that?"

A hesitation, a pause. "Of course not. It's a great deal. Let's move forward. Keep me posted."

Everet wasn't finished. "There's one other thing."

I knew it, I knew it, he thought. Nothing is ever final with Everet.

"What is it, Everet? You want my condo, also?"

"Yeah, maybe. But that's not it. I need to get approval from my client in the US. It should only take a day."

That was new. Was the deal real? What a bastard, Kendrick thought. What was his brother up to now? Maybe Everet really wanted his condo.

He pressed the disconnect button and slammed the phone down on the floor. Everet has screwed him again, he realized. But not for long. This wasn't the end.

Thinking in that vein certainly made him feel better. But he did not know what he should or could do. The story of his life.

Chapter 10

The morning sky was still grey when Kendrick woke up. He had slept little, the thoughts of the deal partnering with his brother repeating in his brain every few moments. Accompanying these thoughts was an image of his bank account and the difficulty of determining where his next dollars were to come from. Bartending barely kept the wolves from the door. That picture also included the images of wife two (Dolores) and three (Melody) and their alimony demands. Whoever wrote the song 'Love For Sale' had little idea of the price. Bitter feelings surfaced in his mind about them and their money grabbing, or was it money grubbing? They wiped him out.

The alarm didn't stop. Get up, it said to him, until he groped for the off button and slammed his fist on the offending timepiece. "God damn it, that hurt," he yelled, as his fist caught the hard edge of the plastic casing. Losing his temper brought him back to the present.

Not all the marriages were a loss, he thought. He reserved a special place in his feelings for number four (Marie) and her untimely death. Other than his parents, it was the first time he had lost someone so dear to him. Even that loss was mitigated somewhat. His daughter, Sandra, was the one bright light in his life.

His struggle out of bed was interrupted by the sound of the 1812 Overture blaring at a high volume in the kitchen. Kendrick ran from the bedroom, picked up the cell phone, and pressed the answer button. It might be something important.

"Is that you, Everet? What's the word?"

"Hi Kendrick, it's Forest. Why did you think I was Everet?"

"Never mind," he heard himself say. Forest ignored the mistake, quickly saying, "Have you heard or seen what's happening downtown?" Forest spoke quickly. No hello, no greeting of any kind, his already high-pitched voice reaching a new height.

"No Forest, should I?"

"Do you recognize the name Rollie Overland?"

"Yeah, of course. He's my brother Everet's son, my nephew. Why do you ask?"

"He's plastering the downtown area with posters. He's sticking them up on every lamp post he could find, every garbage can, every sidewalk bench, even on the doors of all the downtown businesses. Each poster has the councillor faces it with the headline, Who's On The Take? I don't think they can say that."

"Apparently, he already has. Anyway, who's 'they'?"

"It's curious, Kendrick. I never heard of this organization, The Committee For Fair and Responsible Government. What's it all about, Kendrick?"

"You've got me, Forest. Why don't you join and find out instead of asking me? For all you know, Rollie may be competing with the Blue Duck Club for members."

No one would ever give Forest a gold star for creative thinking. "Wow, I never thought of that. Do you think that's what he's up to?"

"Forest, I'm going to take a walk downtown to see this for myself. You're still downtown, right? I'll join you."

Kendrick threw on jeans and a T-shirt, grabbed a light jacket and an umbrella, and took the elevator to the ground floor. "Hi babe," he said to the tired image of the large busted movie starlet on the side of his van, and headed south towards the downtown area, only four blocks away.

It was easy to see where the action was. A phalanx of umbrellas seemed headed for the same destination. When Kendrick reached the umbrella epicentre, there was Forest standing in front of the bank, reading and rereading the poster which someone had plastered on the front window of the bank. It was obviously meant to be noticed, given its size and brilliant red background.

Freddie Gold, the CCSB branch manager, had definitely noticed it. He was standing on the sidewalk, drenched to the skin, trying to pull up one corner of the poster in order to remove it. His futile efforts had attracted the attention of a gaggle of passersby who were eager to read the message before Freddy could remove the offending words. Four feet to the left, Rollie Overland was busy flattening the edge of the same poster to ensure it was adhering to the window.

"Hey Freddie," said Raymond Little, "is the bank sponsoring this movement?" Freddie took a sideways glance at Rollie and the poster before turning to Raymond. "Not on your life, sir. This is a travesty. I'm reporting this to the police. The bank has nothing to do with this."

"So, who's this guy helping you? Is he one of your assistant managers? "

Rollie could easily be mistaken for a bank employees.He wore light brown leather slip-ons, super-slim light grey slacks and a blue dress jacket, no tie. His gold coloured nameplate had his name 'Roland Overland, President' in black. The tattoos were discreetly hidden.

Freddie took another quick glance at Rollie, saw he was putting up the poster, not taking it down, and yelled at him, "Stop that or I'll see that you're never a client of this bank." Rollie gave him the finger.

Like weeds, the rain seemed to promote the growth of the crowd. Despite the increased volume of rain, they appeared unable to tear themselves away from the competing efforts to mount the poster and its headline - "***Who's On The Take?***"

The large white letters on the red background were like a magnet for the eyes. The words provided confirmation of the rumours swirling around the town for years. Their councillors were on the take and also spending the town's money like drunken sailors.

Kendrick and Forest stood next to Oliver Green, Forest's cousin, and Martha, his wife. Despite the inclement weather and under the protection of a large black umbrella, the couple was formally dressed. Oliver in his dark suit and tie and Martha in her print dress, nervously clutching her handbag. Both of them were long-time residents of Port Detour and decried the growth of the town and the change it brought to their childless lives.

"I told you, Martha," Kendrick overheard Oliver say to his wife, "I tried to vote those crooks out of office two years ago. God knows how much they've stolen since then." He added, "We should join and get rid of those commies." Martha looked with concern at her husband.

Forest moved a step closer to the window and put his finger on the words on the poster underneath the screaming headline.

"Are These People To Be Trusted?"

"That what I'm talking about, Kendrick. Those words are inflammatory. Rollie will be sued for defamation."
"Only if it's not true, Forest. Even then, I would imagine a lawsuit would bring even more publicity. This is a US style approach,. Where is it coming from, and how does Rollie know anything about what's happening in Port Detour?"

Below the question on the poster appeared to be mug shots of the mayor and the five town councillors. The images had been altered to appear as images from a police lineup. Each image had the person's name underneath and a number and date styled in a way to give the impression that this was their prison number.

Underneath the images were the words:

"Why Would You Re-Elect the People Who Are Robbing You?"

Our taxes have increased 30% over the past two years, our councillors pocketed a pay increase of 45%, our roads are a disgrace and we have spilled garbage all over our downtown streets.

Stop the theft and incompetence.

Drain the swamp. Send these crooks back to where they came from. Let's take back our town and make Port Detour Great Again.

Join Today.

The last item on the poster was a head shot of Rollie Overland. It was AI enhanced to remove any blemishes and add a perfect smile. The caption read:

Rollie Overland, President
The Committee For Fair and Responsible Government
Your Taxes Well Spent.

"Have you talked to Everet about this?" asked Forest.

Kendrick squinted at Forest and dragged out his cell phone. "I was just going to do that, Forest." He hated it when someone thought faster than he did. After a few minutes of searching his contacts, he found Everet's name and hit the now familiar number. A booming voice, not unlike a TV pitchman, came through the speaker with words of greeting.

"Hey Kendrick, just the man I wanted to talk to. I've put all the information about the land purchase down on paper. It's got everything you need to know about the deal. I'll drop it off at your condo this afternoon. Anyway, why are you calling? Feeling guilty about taking so much money from me? How about we make it twenty-five seventy-five?"

Kendrick felt panic rise inside him. Was his brother serious? He made his voice sound big. "A deal's a deal, Everet. No way I'm agreeing to anything like that."

He could hear a chuckle at the other end. "Just testing, bro. We'll keep the same deal. What did you phone me for?"

"Do you know what your son's doing right now?"

"Well, if he's doing what I did at his age, he's one lucky person. Never can have too many women." His laugh could be heard by anyone standing within twenty feet of the phone. "Good thing I bought him a double bed." The laugh increased in volume. "Why do you ask? Has he got the politicians of Port Detour up in arms yet?"

"Get serious, Everet. He's downtown plastering posters everywhere, criticizing the mayor and the council. He's accusing them of theft. "

Everet's reply was swift. "So? It sounds like the start of a political campaign. The kid's got the gift for it–a big mouth and balls. What about friends? Is there a gang of them?"

Kendrick looked around, but could only recognize the people of Port Detour. He could see Rollie standing, his task completed, the bottom corner of the poster secure. He raised his arms, waved his hands and yelled to the crowd, "Attention, everyone!" Another young man, dressed in neat casual clothes, handed Rollie a microphone and positioned a two-foot speaker close to his right knee. As if on cue, the crowd quieted, and all eyes were on Rollie, who silently and slowly rotated his head and body to view the circle of Port Detour's finest citizns.

The audience was mesmerized. After all, this was a bank. A Canadian bank. Nobody made fun of a bank. Who was this young man? Where was he leading them? How could he say the things listed on the poster? What did he know they didn't?

Freddy Gold stood slack-jawed, looking at the scene unfolding in front of him. 'Why me, Lord, why me?' he seemed to mouth.

Chapter 11

"You're probably wondering what this is all about?" asked Rollie, scanning the crowd. He paused. Nobody said anything.

"So am I. Why is everyone standing around this branch?" He listened to scattered applause. "Maybe they're giving out samples? What do you say, Mr. Gold? Is that right?"

Freddy Gold, now the centre of attention, recalled the nude protest by the Blue Duck group last year. Banks just weren't regarded as good corporate citizens, at least by the people who had been turned down for a loan. He looked at his feet, hoping the sidewalk would open up and swallow him.

Rollie started pacing inside the circle of the crowd. "No, they're not giving out free samples. Our town is just like this bank. All they do is take and give us scraps. What we want to know is where our tax dollars went." Some people moved their head up and down. Rollie's voice increased in volume and his pace quickened. Kendrick thought he recognized the technique. Somebody had trained this young man. He was effective.

The drizzle stopped, and the sky brightened. "Even God is on our side," yelled Rollie, pointing up at the sky. For a church going community like Port Detour, they were conditioned to believe in miracles and a significant number in the crowd nodded their assent.

"I don't have to go into detail," Rollie continued. "The facts are on these posters. Our councillors have been ripping you off for years.

Just look around. Poor roads, run down parks, no snow clearing, all kinds of workers standing around doing nothing. It's a disgrace. Join us and drain the swamp." If anyone recognized the words from south of the border, they didn't say.

A voice cried out from the crowd. "Who are you? Where are you from?"

"Glad you asked," responded Rollie as a few rays of sunlight poked through the clouds.. He pointed upwards. "Here comes the sun and here I am. What a coincidence."

The crowd frowned collectively and then broke into a smile. This could be fun, thought several citizens.

"My name is Rollie Overland and you may know my dad, Everet, and my uncle, Kendrick. They were born and raised in Port Detour and after an absence of forty years, they're ready to retire to the finest community in Canada. I was born here and spent all my summers with my grandparents, so I know Port Detour like the back of my hand. I was educated in the States and worked there until recently. Do you want to know why I say recently?"

Every head bopped up and down.

"The US is like the devil's home. It's evil. I'm back because Port Detour is going the same way. Where do you think all those crazy left-wingers want to come? I want to make sure it doesn't happen. I want to protect Port Detour and keep it a great place for my dad and my uncle and all you fine people gathered here. If we don't do something now, and I mean right now, you won't have a town to live in. I know that. You know that. Elections are coming up in a few weeks and I want to be your mayor. That's how we're going to make Port Detour a great town again and make it the best place for everyone to live in." Rollie paused. "And your taxes will go down. I know how to do that."

That was the magic phrase. Someone cheered, and another voice called out, "I'm with you, Rollie. It's about time."

Rollie reduced his voice to reflect the seriousness of the situation. "I won't bore you with a fancy speech. I just need you to join *The Committee For Fair and Responsible Government* and then vote for me when the election comes around. But enough politicking. I'd like to meet as many of you as I can. Since I will be working for you, you deserve to know who your employee is, so I'm going to stop talking and mingle. I hope you have time to stay around."

He handed the microphone back and turned to meet the people closest to him. With a big smile and an outstretched hand, he dove into the crowd. People appeared to like him. They were also concerned. "Rollie, you can't do this by yourself. Who's running with you?"

"Fred, it is Fred, right? Fred, you would be astonished at the quality of people we have in this town. The old guard buried those up and comers under a rock, you know. They couldn't afford to be challenged, what with all the graft, kickbacks, perks, you name it. No wonder there wasn't any money to make the town work. That's got to change. I've found some really smart people who will make sure it's the citizens who get taken care of, not themselves. You'll meet them at the next candidate's meeting."

The lineup to talk to Rollie grew longer. For everyone wanting to asking a question, ten other people crowded around, listening to the current question and answer.

"And take the police and the firemen. Do you know we have more police and firemen per capita than Toronto.? Imagine that. Everyone earning over one hundred grand a year."

"No way," said an elderly farmer.

"Yes way," said Rollie. He again scanned the crowd. "Anyone here earn over one hundred grand last year?" No one's hand went up.

"I thought so," said Rollie. "You know, they all protect their own. They hand out fancy raises to each other every year. There's nobody to vote against them."

"That'll never change, Rollie," said Myrtle Wright. "No one can stop ……"

Rollie cut her off and leaned in to read Myrtle's nametag. "You have a nametag, Myrtle, so I assume you work at the hospital? I know you and the other nurses are underpaid. That'll change if you vote me and my team into office. We'll fire half those overpaid people before their heads stop spinning. The savings should go to bump up your pay, Myrtle."

Those were magic words. No one had ever said them before, as far as Myrtle could remember. She raised her eyebrows in disbelief and looked at her fellow nurse, Lizzie, standing beside her. "Yeah, sure."

Their union contracts meant Rollie couldn't influence what nurses are paid. Regardless, Rollie pressed on. He wanted votes, whatever he had to say, true or not.

"No Myrtle, I'm going to make it happen. You, of all people, know firsthand how useless most of those managers and supervisors are. Do you think you could do your job without them?"

Now that made sense to Myrtle and her co-worker. She nodded her head, understanding how it might just be possible. She turned to Lizzie, nodded her head, and turned back to Rollie.

"I'm voting for you, Rollie. At last, someone will pay attention to us working folks." She turned to her husband. "You and I are voting together this time, Marvin."

After ten minutes of meet and greet, Rollie again raised his arm and in a loud voice, said, "Next week there's an all candidates meeting at the high school. They've invited all the candidates, including the current councillors, since they are the ones who have got Port Detour in this current mess. Let's ask them some questions."

He looked around to gauge the level of interest. His announcement had generated a lot of discussion. Many people were talking to the person next to them.

"It's on Tuesday at six PM. We need everyone to come out and meet the team and hear just how we are going to reduce your taxes. It's really important. If you don't elect us, just imagine what those thieves will do next. Who will stop them? Thank you."

It took another ten minutes for the crowd to disburse. All they could talk about was Rollie and the windfall he was promising.

Forest had remained in the centre of the crowd and was surprised to hear the positive comments from most of the people, the same people who had voted the current councillors into office. Would they still be in after election day? Not from what he heard.

He had to admit that Rollie had won him over. And another thing. This was be the most important election in years. He personally was going to make sure everyone he knew heard about Rollie and his team. It was time for a change.

Chapter 12

Rey Rey had reverted to style and wore his blackest suit, darkest tie, whitest dress shirt and gravest face. Everyone knew he had a penchant for offside humour and people often-times looked for the display. Today they weren't disappointed. The emerald green socks with white rabbits could be seen with every step. He met the group on the front steps of the Supreme Funeral Home, suitably framed between the large Corinthian pillars supporting the portico and light strains of classical music playing in the background. He always treated every arriving group with reverence and had done this so often that a casual observer could not have detected if he was welcoming a grieving family or the investigative committee of the Blue Duck Social Club.

"Welcome, everyone," he intoned, sweeping his arm in front of him, and trying, without success, to control the smile appearing on his face. "Follow me."

Gail, Emile, Forest, Dakari and Marg arrived on time at two PM, recognizing the solemnity of the meeting location. Punctuality was a habit everyone subscribed to in Port Detour, knowing a funeral ceremony was the last journey for the guest of honour. Their desire for meeting anonymity, at least from Kendrick, was honoured. Nobody had died over the previous two days. They had the place to themselves.

"It's rarely we're here to celebrate the living," said Rey Rey trying to elevate the mood. Must be undertakers' humour, thought Marg.

Rey Rey stopped and with a grand gesture showed the group into a small meeting room off the main hallway. A long cloth-covered table occupied the centre and seats were arranged along both sides of the table. Samuel Barber's Adagio For Strings played softly in the background until Rey Rey moved quickly to flip the off switch.

"Requests anyone?" he asked with an enormous smile, still trying to lighten the mood. "Sit anywhere you want."

As soon as they were seated, a young lady brought in two carafes of coffee and placed them alongside the cups and saucers. She returned shortly with two plates of dainty biscuits and placed them on the table within easy reach of the meeting attendees. Dakari immediately grabbed two chocolate and three vanilla cookies and said, "Excuse me, but I missed lunch today. I went to a meet and greet event at the coffee house this morning. I wanted to find out more about Rollie. Do you know they served nothing?" He looked hurt. "Anyway, let's get going."

Rey Rey wasted no time. "OK folks, I've got our trip planned. Here's the itinerary." He handed out one sheet of paper to each person, waited for the recipients to read the words, and started talking slowly and quietly.

"I've scheduled our trip for five days. First, we'll go to North Bay on day 1 and then to Sudbury for days two and three, then on to Little

Current for a day. I've arranged for accommodation at a local motel in each of the towns. It should be enough time at each place. I think we'll find out as much as we want after we've talked to four or five people."

Dakari leaned forward. "I don't know where you got this estimate, but wouldn't it also depend on what people tell us? It also raises the question: what are we going to ask these informers?"

Rey Rey wasn't to be deterred with such practical matters. His specialty was organization,

"We'll figure that out when we have to, Dakari. What's so difficult about it? Seems simple to me."

Dakari gave up. He decided the group was headed down a one-way path. Nobody thought strategizing or even planning interviews were important.

Rey Rey glanced around the table, seeking nods of approval of his master plan. Satisfied, he then added an afterthought, "Transportation is a problem. We have no way to get there and back."

There was a pause as everyone reached out for another cookie. Marg acted as the host and asked, "More coffee, anyone?"

"How abut we rent a van?" suggested Forest. Silence descended on the group.

"And who's going to pay for it, Forest?" said Dakari. "I've got a better alternative." He leaned forward as if he was going to let them in on a conspiracy. "How about a fishing trip? It makes sense. Northern Ontario, the wilderness, more than one day."

"What on earth are you talking about, Dakari?" asked Gail. "Let's keep on topic."

"I am right on topic. We should ask Kendrick for the loan of his van. It's big enough to accommodate all of us, and a fishing trip is the ideal cover."

The brilliance of the idea was immediately apparent to everyone. "Go for it, Dakari. Ask Kendrick." Dakari didn't hesitate. "Count it done. I'll speak to him today."

The resolution of the transportation problem brought to the fore what were they trying to find out. Forest was the first to bring the subject up. "So, we have accommodation and we'll soon have transportation. Aren't we forgetting two things?"

Rey Rey and the rest of the group, other than Marg, averted their eyes and studied their shoes. Who wants to give an answer that has nothing to do with the question? Let someone else look foolish.

Marg spoke up. "I was thinking the same way, Forest. As Dakari said, how are we going to find someone who knows Kendrick, and what are we going to ask them?"

Forest nodded knowingly, hiding the fact he didn't have a clue how to make it happen.

Nobody noticed Dakari's absence. Suddenly, he appeared in the room's doorway and loudly announced, "We got it." Everyone looked his way. "Kendrick's going to lend us his van. All he asked for was some means of transportation while we're on our fishing trip."

He moved back to his seat at the table.

"You don't have a vehicle, Dakari. How did you arrange a replacement?" said Rey Rey.

"That's was easy, my friend. I said you'd lend him your Corvette while we use his van."

"You did what? Who told you I would lend out my car?"

"You did. Maybe not in so many words, but since you organized the trip, I thought it would be OK. Anyway, that's what he said he wanted. I didn't have a choice."

The quiet ambience of a funeral home was shattered by Rey Rey's shout, "Didn't have a choice? Didn't have a choice? No way. I've had that car for over ten years. It's my baby. Tell him he can't have it."

Dakari didn't react, other than to say, "Too late. He's on his way over here right now to pick it up. What's the big deal? It's only for five days."

"Oh, the five days start now? When were you going to tell us we're leaving tomorrow? Or is it tonight?"

"Let's leave tomorrow. It's too late for today. Give me your keys and I'll meet him at the front."

Rey Rey jumped up so fast he upset his chair on the floor. "He's driving that van with the bikini actress up to our front door? Oh my God, you can't leave it in the driveway overnight. Old Mr. Grant will die."

"Probably not from the van, Rey Rey," said Marg, referring to the funeral home owner. "Maybe we should stick around and see something else rising from the dead when he sees the blond."

"You're sick, Marg." said Rey Rey.

"I'll take care of it," said Dakari. "I'll bring it to my house and pick everyone up tomorrow morning and we'll be off."

Marg raised her hand for attention. "Don't bother picking Emile and I up, Dakari. Someone has to find out more about Everet. Emile's a cop and since we have to go to the States, he'll have more leverage than the rest of us. I'll go with him. Someone has to drive."

She rose. "I have to go pack. Wait a minute. Dakari, you don't own a car. Do you even have a driver's license?"

"No Marg, of course not. I don't need one."

Well, that certainly makes sense, thought Marg. Maybe gaps in logic were the sign of artistic talents. You only need a license when the police stop you.

"Then it's set," said Dakari. "Tomorrow morning Gail, Forest and Rey Rey. First thing, OK? Eleven AM."

Marg almost wished she was going in the van, solely to witness what she knew would be a bizarre experience. Nobody had continued the discussion about how and what information they were going to get. As far as she knew, none of the four had ever been over fifty miles north of Port Detour in their lifetime, and they were being driven there by an artist without a driver's licence.

At least she was with a cop. Emile knew all about investigations, interrogations and had contacts on every police force south of the border. If necessary, she'd even let Emile interview her.

It was thirty minutes before Kendrick showed up. The conversation about Rollie continued, especially about why Rollie was running for mayor. Dakari related Rollie's stock answer about cleaning up the city.

"That's what he said, folks. I'm not sure I believe him. He's just too glib for my taste. I'm sure there's something else, a hidden agenda, but I've no idea what it might be."

Marg paid close attention. She thought Dakari might be right. The saying about a chip off the old block resonated.

As they exited the building, Kendrick drove onto the driveway and parked his van in front of the pillared entrance. He quickly exited the vehicle and bound up the steps to where the group had stopped to witness the arrival of the bikini-clad model.

"Where are the keys, Rey Rey?" he immediately asked.

Rey Rey took his time pretending to search for the Corvette keys, extracted them from his shirt pocket and slowly handed them over. Kendrick grabbed the keys before Rey Rey could change his mind and remarked, "I've owned three of these. It'll be just like old times."

Rey Rey reacted to the reference, remembering Kendrick's no risk attitude to life when he was a teenager.

"Remember, no racing."

It was doubtful he heard him. Kendrick, his eyes firmly fixed on the Corvette parked by itself in the farthest corner of the lot, moved at speed, the benefit of having very long legs. Emile watched Kendrick dash away and then turned to Marg.

"Hey Marg, I think I know how we can easily find out about Everet's forty lost years." Previous comments abut how to do so seemed to have disappeared from his mind. "My instincts tell me there's more than meets the eye with him. I bet he's left a trail even a kid could follow. Dollars to doughnuts he has a police rap sheet."

The revving sound of the Corvette engine drowned out their conversation, and they both turned to see the low slung vehicle leap from its parking spot. When it reached them, the car was a red blur as it rocketed across the parking lot and onto the street.

Rey Rey watched the car flash past, raised his hands and yelled out to no one in particular, "What's he doing? He's going to crash. That's my baby."

"Relax Rey Rey. All he's doing is driving fast," said Marg, a broad smile on her face. "What were you saying, Emile? I couldn't hear for the noise. Just how are you going to do that?"

They didn't see Rey Rey's shoulders collapse, but they heard his concern. "Is this how he's going to drive when we are away? I want my car back." He realized the impossibility of that happening with a question to Dakari. "Can you give me a ride home?"

Marg, Emile, Dakari and Rey Rey reached the bottom of the steps and were still gazing in astonishment at the taillights of the Corvette as it fishtailed out of the parking lot onto Elm Street.

They were immediately distracted by another occurrence. Marg and Emile were on the outside of the group and heard the roar of a gunned engine immediately behind them, coming from the far reaches of the parking lot. Emile managed a quick backward look, quickly grabbed Marg by her arm and yelled, "Watch out Marg, you're going to get hit."

He roughly hauled her down to the pavement, her fall broken by Emile's body now lying prone on the pavement, over three feet away from where they were standing. As they hit the ground, a dark-coloured sedan roared by, narrowly missing both of them and continued to accelerate towards the exit. Rey Rey and Dakari quickly ran back, bent down and helped the two to their feer. Marg's hair had shaken loose and Emile's clothes looked like someone who had rolled in a dirt pile.

"What the hell was that?" asked Rey Rey. "Are you two OK?"

Emile dusted himself off, looked at the other three and without hesitation, said, "That, my friends, was a deliberate attempt at a hit and run. Someone wants to kill me."

"You can't be serious," said Dakari. "The guy driving that car was distracted and driving much too fast. Did you not see him swerve right after he nearly hit you? He was probably on his phone. You're imagining things …."

Emile cut him off, sweat now showing on his brow and his nostrils flaring. His fists were clenched, and he shook one fist in Dakari's face. "You do not know what you're talking about, Dakari. I've been targeted before. Have you?"

Dakari stepped back. "No, of course not. But you're right Emile. You're the cop, not me. Did you see the driver's face?"

"Did you, Dakari? You were with us. Surely you saw the driver's face clearly, you being an observant artist. Well?" It came out as a challenge. Emile immediately felt bad. It wasn't Dakari's fault. He wasn't the one targeted.

"I'm sorry, Dakari. That shook me up a bit. Are you OK Marg?"

Everyone looked at Marg, who had finished rearranging her wardrobe.

"In my career, I've been threatened more times than I can count. If you're right Emile, and I'm not questioning your conclusion, it doesn't bother me too much. Any threats I've received have been because someone's angry. This is different. Why would somebody want to run me down? No Emile, it must be you. You've arrested one person too many, apparently." She smiled. "Although I have to ask, why? But only you can answer it, Emile. Who did you last shake down?"

"Marg, I never …" He stopped mid sentence, realizing Marg was kidding. "But this is serious, Marg. It isn't every day when somebody wants to kill a cop. Anyway, I've always been Mr. Nice Guy, so I'll be serious and so should you. Maybe it isn't me they're after, Marg, it's you. But the guy is gone, so we have nothing to work with. Let's go back to what we were doing. If he wants to kill you, he'll show up again."

"Gee, thanks Emile. I can hardly wait. But I think you're wrong. Why would anyone be after me? I haven't lived here for forty years, nor have I worked here. No, it's you Emile."

In the turmoil, Rey Rey hadn't received an answer about Dakari giving him a ride home.

"What about it, Dakari, can you give me a lift?"

"Sure, Rey Rey. Hop in," said Dakari, fingering the van keys with the red pompom on the end of the key chain. He and Rey Rey entered Kendrick's van. Dakari, after some searching, started the engine. The exhaust pipe expelled an enormous cloud of blue smoke and the van roared off as if in pursuit of the red Corvette. Now Rey Rey's eyes were fixed on Dakari, wide open in alarm.

Chapter 13

Emile and Marg were left standing in the parking lot, alone. Marg always hated a vacuum, but the words that popped out surprised her. She had never made overtures to men, only this one.

"Hey, Emile, since we're in this together, how about you tell me your plan over supper and a good bottle of red? I could whip up a quick meal for us, something simple like spaghetti and garlic bread with a Caesar salad,"

Emile stared at Marg, seemingly not knowing how to handle this personal invitation. He hadn't had a date in decades. But she must be serious. The menu appeared more than simple.

"Well, I'm not going to bite your head off, Emile. Do you want to be wined and dined by the only femme fatale you know?"

Emile finally managed a reply.

"If that's simple, then I'm in. What time?"

"Seven, OK?"

Emile nodded yes. "I have to go, Marg. I have one errand to run." With that brief explanation, he hurried off, leaving Marg standing alone on the steps.

"What did I say?" she said in a low voice to no one. She thought he looked like a panicked rabbit, given the speed of his departure. His car flashed past, Emile's eyes straight ahead.

Marg picked up the supplies for supper and was home within a half hour, debating what to wear. She and Emile had primarily dealt with the low life of the world in their careers. It was time to change the game. It was time to show she had a soft and sophisticated side to her. She wanted to impress Emile, but not to the point of scaring him away. Black is good, she thought, all black with a string of pearls.

Emile rang the buzzer from the condo lobby at precisely seven o'clock and was at her entrance in seconds, proffering a bouquet of mixed flowers. She thought of the old cliche. Great minds think alike.

"My, my Emile, I appreciate it, but you didn't have to go to that much trouble. A suit and tie yet. You look like you're going to a formal ball and all I'm serving is spaghetti."

Emile's face was a blank as he admitted, "I don't get out much, Marg. Not since Gladys died. This is a real treat. Thanks for inviting me."

Ten minutes later, he said, "Marg, this is excellent." Emile's smile was constant throughout the meal. Sixty minutes later, he drank the last of the wine in his glass, arranged his fork and knife carefully on the empty plate, and rested his elbows on the table.

"That was fabulous, Marg. You have a hidden talent."

A little too effusive, thought Marg. Maybe she wasn't the only one trying to make an impression.

Both had enjoyed the small talk and bantering, each telling tales of criminals they knew who had made the Darwin Awards. As she cleared the dishes, her lawyer's mind returned. "OK Emil, what's the master plan?"

"Marg, there's no need to go on a road trip like the other group. We can get information about Everet without leaving Port Detour. All I have to do is make a few phone calls to my police buddies in the States. If he's done anything illegal, it'll be recorded somewhere."

"That's fantastic, Emile," said Marg, trying to hide her disappointment about the aborted trip. "When can you call them?"

"As soon as I get home, Marg." He looked at his watch. "Wow, I didn't mean to keep you up so late. I should go. I'll call when I hear something."

Emile hurriedly got up and was gone within minutes. He's nervous, thought Marg. He hasn't been alone with another woman for years. Marg wasn't far behind Emile. Twenty minutes later, she was sound asleep.

She woke early and lingered over her coffee while seated at the kitchen table, her cell phone nearby. At nine, her cell phone played its familiar call tune. She waited for five rings before answering.

Her excitement rapidly died. "No, I don't need any duct cleaning. How did you get this number, anyway?" Still no call from Emile.

At noon, her condo buzzer sounded. Marg was pleasantly surprised to hear Emile's voice on the intercom.

"Can I come up, Marg? I've got something."

Emile walked in looking like he had just been to his personal groomer. He wore black patent leather loafers, black jeans and a white open-neck shirt with the sleeves turned up. But it was his face that Marg noticed the most. He had a mile wide grin. In each hand, he held a paper bag displaying the name of the local high class bistro.

"Which one do you want? Croque Monsieur or Croque Madame?"

"Monsieur, of course, mon chef. I've read about the cops and their fondness for coffee shops, Emile. But this is over the top." Emile again broke into a smile. My God, the man smiles a lot, thought Marg. She arranged the kitchen table, made coffee and put the sandwiches on plates. "So what's the something? What have you found?"

Emile took a large bite of his sandwich, chewed and swallowed quickly and announced, "Start packing, Marg. We're going on a mission to Syracuse to see my buddy Spike."

"Spike? you have a friend called Spike? What breed is he?"

She laughed but noticed Emil had had a puzzled look on his face.

"It's a joke, Emile. Anyway, what did your friend find?"

"Marg, what he found you won't believe. But it's confidential, even by police standards. In fact, it's so confidential he'll only show it to me. No sending it by email." He looked at her and continued. "He said that he might be able to make a copy."

"That doesn't make sense, Emile. You said he would only show it to you and now you're saying the bulldog will make a copy. Which way is it?"

"He's going to make a copy tonight, after everyone has left. That's what he'll give me. It's against policy, Marg, so we owe him big time. I'll have to figure out a way to repay him. There's one other thing."

Marg looked at him and said nothing, not rising to the bait.

"We've got to travel. Spike is at the FBI field office in Syracuse."

That required a response, since Emile was not entirely forthcoming. Was this overnight? Was this the royal 'we' or did he mean himself only? Why not be daring? Go for it, she thought.

"Are you asking me if I'll go the Syracuse with you, Emile? Sure, why not?"

Emile's shoulders relaxed a little, his eyes brightened, a modest smile appeared and his response was not the typical Emile she knew. He was demonstrably excited.

"Alright!" He looked at the time on his watch and said, "Finish your sandwich and throw some clothes in a travelling bag. We'll take my car. I've got everything I need in the car."

"You smoothy," said Marg. Emile beamed.

Chapter 14

Five hours later, after clearing customs and immigration at Watertown, they pulled in to the parking lot of the downtown Holiday Inn. It was close to seven o'clock.

"A double room, please, two single beds," Marg told the clerk. "One night."

Emile hung back and put away his credit card. He didn't see what Marg had written on the registration card. The clerk said, "Room 461, fourth floor. The elevators are right behind me."

On the fourth floor, Marg scanned the keyless card, opened the door and marched in. "Left or right bed, Emile?" His attempt at nonchalance was futile when the suitcase he threw on the left bed slid over the edge and ended up on the floor.

"What about supper, Marg? I'm tired. Is the hotel dining room OK?"

The rest of the evening went by quickly. Marg thoroughly enjoyed the conversation. The martinis had their effect; the meal was passable, and they were back in the room by nine thirty.

Emile seemed nervous. Sitting in the lone upholstered chair, he crossed and uncrossed his legs and his conversation was of nothing. Marg finally had enough.

"Look Emile, we're two older people sharing a hotel room. Period. Hopefully, you aren't thinking about sex, because I'm certainly not."

"Certainly not, Marg." He regretted the phrasing and tried to make amends. "Not that you aren't attractive, Marg. It's just that… " His voice trailed off to a whisper.

"Yes, go on Emile. I know your wife died three years ago, so I can understand. Anyway, sex to me is a foreign land. Not that I don't like it, but the situation has to be right. This isn't right. OK?"

Emile seemed relieved. "Not a problem, Marg. I'd like to get some sleep. It's been a long day."

Marg made no move to get up from the edge of the bed where she was sitting. "Emile, I've got to tell you something before this investigation goes too far."

Emile relaxed. He'd heard a lot of confessions in his time. He was on firm ground here. "What on earth are you talking about, Marg? What do you know?"

"Emile, long before you came along, in fact when I was eighteen, our high school graduating class had a party at one of the kids' house. A rich guy. Swimming pool catered food and access to his dad's booze. Anyway, I had too much to drink and was completely sloshed. A guy invited me upstairs to a bedroom, and I stupidly agreed. After all, I was an adult now. What could happen that I didn't have control over?"

Emile the cop sat quietly. He'd heard this sort of thing many times before.

"Anyway, the guy wouldn't stop and nobody could hear me yelling for help. Not that it would matter. He held me down and his brother helped him. I was raped, Emile. Raped."

"That's terrible Marg. Did you ever tell anyone?"

"How could I, Emile? In those days, it was always the girl's fault. No, I said nothing. You're the first person I've ever told."

Emile sensed there was more. "Go on, Marg. That wasn't the end, was it? It never is."

"You're right. I turned into a frigid sex partner with most everyone I met. A few times it was great, with the right guy and the right setting. But sex is something I avoid, Emile. Do you understand?"

"I sure do, Marg. Remember, I'm a cop. I've heard your story dozens of times. It's not your fault. And about the not telling, it's good that you have. It won't remove the memory or the trauma, but you'll feel better for telling,"

Marg was softly crying now and Emile got up, sat beside her on the bed and held her close. She didn't object.

"Care to tell me who the guys were? Perhaps we should try to punish them, even though it's forty years later."

"Oh, they'll get their punishment, Emile. I'll see to that. In fact, that's why I had to tell you. I didn't want you to think I was angry for no reason."

"Angry? You have a right to be angry. Who were these creeps?"

Marg hesitated. What trouble was she going to get them in? What if she had to go public in order to make it right? What additional memories might be recalled by revealing the names?

"You probably have a good idea who they were, Emile. I can't ever be courteous to those two, and I think it shows."

Marg could see Emile racking his brain. He hadn't been around forty years ago and wouldn't have known all the players.

"Marg, are you concerned nobody will believe you?"

Marg had never thought about that. That was a possibility, something she wasn't prepared to undergo.

"I'd prefer not to let anyone know, Emile. Not at this time. Maybe later. It's a big step for me just to admit it to another person, much less the entire world. Leave it with me, please."

Emile loosened his hug, held her by the shoulders to face him, and spoke softly.

"Marg, whatever you decide is OK with me. I'll tell no one, nor do I think you did anything wrong. As far as I'm concerned, you were physically assaulted. The rape has only made it worse. Men like that should be brought to justice. You've got my full support."

"Well, Emile, your support won't help. Those two will get their punishment, and I'm just the person to do so. Forty years in the criminal justice system teaches you a lot and the thing I've found is not to be sympathetic to criminals. Those two are going to suffer, just as much as I have."

Emile couldn't help but notice how hard her face had become. She wasn't even looking at him, just staring off into the void. What could she possibly have in mind? The candidates who popped into his mind were the Overland brothers. Same school, nearly the same ages.

It wasn't much of a stretch to point the finger at those two. He would have his confrontation with them at a future time.

Chapter 15

It was six o'clock and Kendrick had just arrived home. He looked at his cell phone. No messages. He called up his name directory and pressed Everet's number.

"What do you want, Kendrick?"

"Everet, it's been two days, and I have heard nothing from you about our little deal. What's up?"

"Not to worry, bro. The deal's solid. Just waiting for an approval from the big guy in the States."

Kendrick mentally added up his debts. They weren't getting smaller and selling the condo would hurt. Everet said 'not to worry', but Kendrick was worried.

His brother had no reason to be worried. Everet looked down at his cell phone and ran down the list of SMS messages. One stood out. "Go ahead," it stated. There was no author name, but the sending number was a 315 area code. Syracuse.

Let him sweat for a day or two, thought Everet. Maybe he could extract a larger share.

Chapter 16

Marg lay in bed, eyes wide open. It was kind of exciting, stealing away like this and in a hotel room in Syracuse with a man she hardly knew. She reviewed the day in her mind and was bothered by a conversation they had shortly after leaving her condo. They had been travelling east on King Street to the expressway, destination Syracuse. Marg turned to Emile and remarked. "Waste of money, don't you think?"

There were political signs everywhere–people's lawns, storefronts, even the enormous billboards at the east end of town. Marg pointed to a lawn crowded with what appeared to be signs for every candidate running for council. A great number of small yellow signs appeared to dominate, advertising an all candidates meeting tonight.

Emile had said nothing, concentrating on the road. Marg let it go. It was just chitchat. Now it bothered her. Maybe it was Rollie's involvement. Why was he running?

Marg turned to see if Emile had fallen asleep. It was hard to tell, no snoring. She took a chance and spoke.

"Emile, are you awake?"

"Yes, what about you?" he laughed. "Why do you ask?"

"I mentioned this afternoon, on the way, that all those political signs were a waste of money. You never answered me. What do you really think?"

"It's a brilliant investment if you're elected, Marg. You'd be surprised what opportunities come to elected officials."

"What are you hinting at, Emile? Are you telling me elected officials are on the take?"

The ex-police officer raised himself on his elbow and looked at her sideways, eyebrows raised. "Marg, it's never that crass. Let's just say that opportunities arise that don't seem to be available to most of us. Nothing illegal, you understand."

"Sure. That's what all my clients told me."

He continued, "One has to wonder who stands to gain the most from this election? The new mayor, a new councilman, the head of the school board? Take your pick."

"I'm glad we're not there Emile. Any contact I've had with politicians reinforces my opinion of them. I suppose it's interesting what they say, but few follow through on their promises. They all have hidden agendas."

"I'll second that, counsellor. Perhaps there'll be fireworks tonight, what with that new young guy running for mayor."

"Rollie Overland? He's a kid, Emile. He's going to be eaten alive by the old guard."

At seven o'clock, all the chairs in the Port Detour high school gym were occupied, many by members from the Blue Duck Social Club, and people started standing along the walls. On the stage were a dozen empty chairs flanking the speaker's podium.

At the back wall, under the folded-up basketball hoop, an enormous banner stretched across the olive green background with the words ***The Committee For Fair and Responsible Government - Your Taxes Well Spent.***

Underneath the banner, Rollie Overland was conferring with six people, all his age or a little older. They had one thing in common. Their arms and parts of their necks were crowded with tattoos. Images of snakes, stars, marijuana plants and red hearts were favourites. Contrastingly, the young men were clean shaven. Rollie stood out in a dark blue suit with narrow pant legs, new white sneakers and an open neck white dress shirt.

"OK, you know your roles, right?" He looked directly at three of them. "Gabe, Rosalynn and Moses stand along the wall where everyone can see you. But not near each other. Say hello to as many people as possible. Make it look like you're from Port Detour. Make friends. Gabe, I'm a little worried about your question. Don't make it too aggressive, just a normal query from a resident. Remember, we want to highlight the non-actions of the councillors, but also attack them as incompetent and on the take. OK?"

Gabe, Rosalynn, and Moses nodded in agreement. "OK, you three, off you go. Find positions near the back so everyone will be curious and look back at you when you have a question."

He then turned to the other three people. Their T-shirts were decidedly more conservative than the first three. The branding on the men's shirts were all recognizable - Gap, Old Navy and Levi's. The Port Detour Community Centre, with its hangout coffee shop, had been a great place to recruit like-minded people.

"You each know your scripts, right?" They nodded yes. "When we go on the stage, please sit to the left of the podium. We're a team. You'll be asked questions but do not, I repeat, do not go off script. We want to get elected, not lead a cause."

As they left, he fist bumped with Ron, Isaac and Emerald Rose. "Let's go, guys. Put your jackets on, make sure your tats are covered. We're on."

The MC on the stage, local broadcaster Ricky Walton, could be heard asking the crowd to welcome the candidates for council. Rollie led his group from the back, mounted the stage steps and sat closest to the podium, his three candidates to his left.

The crowd's view was of four people who couldn't have been older than thirty years, Ron, with his long, neatly kept hair. Isaac, whose head was shaved bald, and Emerald Rose, the only female candidate. Their dress was a mixture. Jeans, khakis, sandals and running shoes. The men wore a cotton jacket over their T-shirts. Emerald Rose was dressed in no-nonsense clothes. She wore a subdued red blouse and faded blue jeans. She was a pretty woman but had pulled her hair back in a manner which successfully disguised her good looks, implying seriousness and intelligence. So she hoped. Her wireless rimmed glasses gave her a schoolteacher, or even an environmentalist, look.

Rollie smoothed back his hair and smiled, prompting a comment from one person in the front row who turned to his companion and, in a loud voice, said, "Finally, a guy who looks competent." Rollie overhead the comment and mentally agreed.

Ricky stepped up to the mic. "Welcome everyone. It's great to see such a turnout. For those of you who don't know me, I'm Ricky Walton from the Port Detour Times. Let's not waste any time. Perhaps you gentlemen and the ladies can state your name and a few words about who you are. Here's our first candidate, Rollie Overland."

Rollie was instantly on his feet. He moved to the podium, scanned the crowd, and said, "I'll be quick and to the point. I'm a no-nonsense guy and I'm also I'm a native of Port Detour, born and bred in this community. I've just moved back after twenty years in the US and I want to make Port Detour my permanent home. But I have concerns. Is Port Detour going to turn into USA north? Is everyone going to carry guns? Do the rich people want to bury us normal citizens in poverty and keep all the wealth for themselves?"

His voice rose a notch. "Not if I have any say. Not like our existing do nothing, say nothing councillors." The sound from the crowd reduced notably, and the fidgeting stopped.

He turned to his left and pointed at the other candidates, four men and a woman. Three of them, Fred Percival, John Lubenko and Steve Mertz, looked like the mannequins in the window of Ron's Smart Clothes, dressed in dark suits and white shirts and ties. The existing councillors.

Rollie's face changed to surprise when the longest serving councillor, Fred Percival, took a short step forward and shook Rollie's hand. Rollie barely acknowledged it, touching the councillor's hand as if he'd contract a deadly virus. The crowd started clapping. Rollie turned to face the audience and spoke. He paused in mid-sentence. They weren't clapping for him; they were acknowledging Fred. It went on for three minutes until Fred motioned for them to stop.

Rollie continued on, less confidence apparent in his tone.

"Let's get to the genuine issues in Port Detour. You must have the same concerns I have about the future of our community. I'm here to let you know that with your help we can fix everything and make Port Detour the town it used to be." He paused. "Remember when life in Port Detour was safe and predictable, when your children could go wherever they wanted without you wondering if they would come back? I can make that happen again."

Some attendees in the gym nodded their heads.

"I think I know what your thoughts are. You're thinking, how can such a young and probably inexperienced person like this guy possibly know what Port Detour used to be like and what it needs right now?"

He looked directly at a few faces in the front row and then scanned the room. His Toastmasters experience showed through. Engage your audience, he had learned.

"I may be young, but I know what happens when taxes go up and services go down. I know how it feels to be concerned or even afraid to walk down the streets after dark. I know what happens when a bunch of dopeheads are allowed to occupy our parks. These are dangerous people. Why are they here? Where are our police?" A pause.

With a sweep of his hand towards the three councillors, he said, "Why don't our councillors put a stop to this?"

He scanned the room, making eye contact with a dozen people. Some people nodded their heads. Most didn't.

"Just think about it. Nothing these men have done in real life has prepared them to run a government. They need leadership and guidance. Above all, they need to connect with the people of Port Detour, not ignore us. Unless we take action as loyal, hard-working citizens, we'll become a town that's no different from one south of the border. What a travesty that is. What we need is a new mayor and council."

Rollie stepped back to the podium. The audience was completely quiet. No whispered comments and no applause. The incumbents on stage stared straight at him until Fred slowly stood up, buttoned his suit jacket and, in a loud, booming voice, spoke from where he was standing.

"My young friend here does not differ from a lot of other young people. They rarely let facts impede their opinions. You've known me for over eight years as your councillor. Do you really think that Rollie and his young friends know what they are talking about? Newcomers, outsiders, the three of them. What do they know about Port Detour? I'm sure they know where every tattoo parlour and bar is, but do they know us? Do they know what makes this town tick? I, for one, would hate to see our way of life destroyed and I'm sure John and Steve," he waved his arm at the two other councillors, "think the same way. Do you really think that any of this nonsense he's spouting is true? He refers to south of the border. Sound to me like he's been in La La land too long."

He stopped talking and swung his gaze around the gym. There was complete silence.

"Maybe, just maybe, he wants to turn Port Detour into a branch of the USA and he's going to be the dictator. We've seen what's happened there. Don't let it happen to Port Detour."

He sat down. The crowd erupted with applause. Then they stood and began chanting three names, "Fred, John, Steve".

Rollie was speechless, hanging on to the lectern as if it were a lifeboat. How could he make such a blunder? Who knew Fred could be so effective? All he could think of now was how to salvage the situation. In the back of his mind was the reason he was running for the mayor's position.

This was not going well. His father would not be happy.

Rollie replied with an apology, dripping with sarcasm. "Thanks for the insight, Fred. It's interesting you didn't bring up the solutions to the problems."

Fred just smiled, looked at Rollie and then out to the sea of people clapping in appreciation and even affection.

Stupid. Stupid, he thought. How was he going to correct this?

Ricky was back at the podium.

"Remember, folks, we're having another one of these all-candidates meeting in two weeks and then the election is the week after. Next time, we'll take questions from the floor."

Rollie walked off the stage, his three candidates following like a line of ducks. He didn't say a word to them. What went wrong? He thought a little further about his failure. His father had warned him.

"You're arrogant, Rollie. It'll bite you in the ass. Just make sure it's not my ass, kid."

The three helpers Rollie sent out in the audience were disappointed. Every one an aspiring actor, recruited by Rollie, their acting debut cut off even before the curtain rose. There was nothing to do except leave. As they crossed the high school parking lot, Rollie called out from the open window of his leased white pickup.

"Over here, guys."

He waited for them to be alongside and spoke quickly, trying to avoid anyone seeing the connection.

"Sorry about that, guys. Keep the money, my gift. Anyway, you have exactly the same gig coming up in two weeks. We'll get together and review your roles before then."

The tinted window closed up, and the truck drove off. Before the front wheels hit the street, Rollie dialled a number.

"Dad, it didn't go well. I need some help."

There was a pause and then Rollie continued, "I know, I know. My second big mistake. Don't rub it in. Your place in an hour? Got it."

Chapter 17

That same morning, Gail and Forest stood in the lobby of Gail's condo in a near panic. They stepped back from the plate-glass windows.

They first heard and then saw a large cube van driving erratically through the parking lot, missing a row of parked cars by inches. The driver wore a multi coloured kufu hat and his eyes darted here and there. It was difficult to determine if he was watching for fast moving but unseen vehicles or was he having a panic attack?

The van stopped with a screech of brakes, the buxom starlet in a bikini painted on the side perfectly lined up with the front doors of the condo. Wary, as if the van might move again, they emerged in the sunlight just as the van's passenger side door swung open to reveal Rey Rey, dressed in casual but sombre clothes. His head was shaking, but his face changed from tension to relaxation once he saw Gail and Forest.

Rey Rey spoke with a slight tremble in his voice, "Hi guys, come on in, there's lots of room. Forest, why don't you sit in the passenger seat and Gail and I will sit in the back."

"Hi folks," said Dakari from behind the wheel. "Sorry I'm a bit late, but I had a hard time figuring out the stick shift in this beast. Got it mastered now. Where are your bags?"

Forest looked at Gail. "Forgot them completely, Dakari. Good catch." He was going to add that he was sidetracked by the dramatic entrance of the van, but perhaps Dakari thought it was normal. Saying nothing, he stepped out of the van, retrieved the bags from the lobby, stowed them in the vehicle's rear and sat back down in the passenger seat. "We're off."

There was a momentary grinding of gears until the van pulled forward and out to the street. Luckily there was no oncoming traffic, not that Dakari would know, continuously glancing right and left going through the parking lot exit. There was little conversation in the cab, each person steeling themselves for, in their minds, the inevitable collision.

Gail leaned over and whispered in Forest's ear. "Why is Dakari driving? This isn't safe."

Forest shrugged. "Hey, Dakari. Are you OK driving this beast? Do you want one of us to drive instead?"

"No, I'm great Forest. I love driving. I can see everything there is to see. You know artists. We observe the world and interpret it in our art. I wouldn't give this up for anything."

Forest leaned over to Gail and spoke softly. "No one wanted to drive, Gail. I know you don't know how to drive a truck, but even though Rey Rey or I could drive it, we really didn't want to. Rey Rey and I declined first, without thinking. That left Dakari and he jumped at the chance. He thinks it's an adventure, an experience that will influence his art. Look, I know he's driven before, even if he doesn't have a license. If it gets too dangerous, we'll say so and suggest one of us take over." Gail unclutched her hands, somewhat mollified.

Once on the road, Dakari guided the vehicle with growing confidence, making lane transitions without mishap and smiling broadly as other drivers pulled alongside, perhaps expecting to see the real starlet behind the wheel in her bikini.

"There it is," shouted Dakari, pointing at the exit sign for the expressway north to their first destination, North Bay. Gail leaned over to whisper in Rey Rey's ear, "Rey Rey, tell him–two hands on the wheel."

Rey Rey kept his focus on Dakari. "No, Gail, let's not distract him. We're doing fine now. Remember, we've still got three hours before we get there. I'm more worried about my Corvette. Do you know what kind of driver Kendrick is?"

"All I know, Rey Rey, is how well his brother took care of this van. You tell me what you think."

He looked around the van. "Well, it looks fine. Clean, no garbage. And he must be a careful driver to keep the van for so many years."

"So relax Rey Rey. Although, he's probably never had a sports car before. Who knows what that's done to his sense of adventure? How fast do you think your car can go?"

Rey Rey's eyes opened wide.

"I don't know, Gail. I've never had it over sixty miles per hour." He paused. "My God, the speedometer goes to one-eighty. Do you think he might go for it?" His shoulders slumped, he stared into nothing and sunk back into the seat. Nobody said anything.

Fifteen minutes later, Dakari spoke up, penetrating the silence that had descended on the group. "I gotta go." As if a prayer had been answered, the four-lane expressway heading north displayed a sign, 'Service Centre 5K' prompting a response from Dakari. "Thank God."

Dakari drove the van into the service centre, ignored the speed limit caution, and, as usual, came to a stop in the No-Parking zone exactly in front of the entrance. He bounced out of the van and made a running dash for the door. The other three walked into the food area, bought coffee, and returned to the van. Dakari followed almost immediately, positioned himself back in the driver's seat and started backing the van out of the parking space.

"Hey, Dakari," asked Gail, "how much gas did Kendrick leave in this rattletrap?"

Dakari began the search for the gauge until Forest grew tired of the game and pointed to the nearly empty gauge. "Pull over to the pumps Dakari, it's refuel time." Dakari did as told, opened the door and they could hear him fumbling with the filling door and then inserting the pump handle into the opening.

"Hey guys," he called out, "We're in luck. I just found a pump which has gas on sale. Ten cents cheaper than the next one." They could hear the fuel being pumped into the tank.

In what could only be described as panic mode, Rey Rey opened his door, literally jumped out of the van, ran and grabbed the pump from an astonished Dakari, and yelled, "Stop, stop!"

Dakari fought back. "What do you think you're doing, Rey Rey? Have you gone mad?"

"You're pumping diesel, Dakari, not gas. That's why it's cheaper than the next pump. How much have you put in?"

Dakari frowned, and then his face brightened. "Oh, I get it. You can't mix diesel with gas. It's OK, I just started. We're good."

Rey Rey didn't know how he could say that, but thought to himself that the damage was already done and if it was only a few ounces, it might not matter. And it didn't matter. A cloud of blue smoke poured out of the exhaust five minutes later and then stopped, the engine running smoother than when they first left. Dakari didn't notice.

Gail and Rey Rey were relieved that the engine even started and, once underway, were relaxed enough to converse. Gail turned to Rey Rey.

"We've never talked, Rey Rey. I know you were an undertaker. But who is the real Rey Rey?"

The van swerved violently. "Dakari, keep your eyes on the road," said Forest.

Dakari ignored him. "Hey, guys. I know walking down memory lane is fun, but shouldn't our priority be how we're going to find information about Kendrick?" said Dakari, as he turned to look at his passengers in the front and rear seats.

"But you're right. We need a plan. Let's think about it while we hear from Rey Rey."

"There's not much to tell, Gail. I didn't choose the most exciting business to work in. It was the same routine each day. You know, pick up a body, embalm, dress the corpse, and set up the receiving room for the family. That's it."

Dakari and Forest could easily hear the conversation in the back. Dakari asked, "Yeah, Rey Rey, we know you worked as an undertaker. In high school, you and Forest were like nerds. You know, horn-rim glasses, pens in the shirt pocket. What changed for you to go into such an exciting business?"

"It was consistent, guys. No surprises. I found I didn't like change, so I stayed there for forty years. As to exciting, I bought myself that red Corvette. Now that is exciting."

"Sixty miles an hour. That's exciting?" exclaimed Dakari. Everyone laughed, including Rey Rey.

The conversation opened up a virtual flood of questions. Everyone asked questions of each other. The idea of a plan continued to be submerged. Everyone realized that creating a plan was hard work. Where to start? Procrastination was much easier. Dakari's frown was not seen or possibly ignored by the other passengers. The inquiry continued.

"What about you, Forest?"

"An alcoholic and a master birdhouse builder. That's me." There was silence for a lengthy period. Then, Forest's question broke the quiet.

"You must have had a wild life in Toronto, Gail?" From the raised eyebrow look on the other faces, nobody expected her answer. "I loved my career, but …" Her voice trailed off. She continued, "But the love didn't transfer into my marriage. I had an unhappy, but lucrative marriage, and no sex." Forest wondered where his own partner had acquired the urge so late in life. He had a hard time keeping up.

Forest, not wanting to be categorized as an adult nerd, commented that Dakari's paintings and sculptures were something he aspired to, but family life always got in the way. Everyone looked at him curiously.

The hours flew by, everyone avoiding talking about a way to get the low-down on Kendrick. Dakari's fingers increased their drumming intensity on the wheel with every kilometre covered. Finally, Dakari spotted a sign saying North Bay, six kilometres.

"So, what's the plan, guys?" asked Rey Rey. Everyone looked at everyone else. It was obvious there was no plan.

"I asked right at the beginning, but nobody wanted to discuss it," said Dakari.

"There's where we want to be," Gail called out, pointing to an enormous parking lot with a Walmart anchoring one end. Dakari navigated the van to a far corner of the parking lot, parked reasonably close to one of the painted parking spot lines, making sure that the bikini-clad starlet faced the store.

"What now?" asked Forest. "Why did you want to park here, Gail?"

"Lots of people, Forest, that's why. Some of them are bound to know Kendrick."

Dakari rolled his eyes.

Rey Rey assumed the role of expedition leader and spoke up. "Let's set up one of the folding tables beside the van, pullout the awning and wait for a customer. In the meantime, I'm going to the police station and enquire about Kendrick. I'll find out at Walmart where the station is, take a taxi over to it and be back in an hour."

It was four in the afternoon when Rey Rey reappeared. He knocked on the van door, pulled it open, and entered. His three companions were dead. Dead asleep on the air mattresses they had wisely purchased during his absence. "Rise and shine. Time to regroup."

It didn't take long. Nobody at the police station had heard of someone called Kendrick Overland, nor had anyone come calling to the van. It was time to find a motel for the night. Maybe Sudbury would reveal more. It was much bigger than North Bay, and Kendrick had been a permanent resident in the winter.

"Something's wrong," said Gail. "You can't be in women's clothing sales for forty years and not be known."

Chapter 18

The knock on the door filled one room of the old mansion on Charles Street in Port Detour. The owners had taken great pains redecorating the house and furnishing its rooms with superb artwork and period furniture. As befitting a top-rated B&B, the daily rates reflected its sophisticated accommodations. Everything was exactly in line with Everet's standards, although the money side presented some difficulties. But he needed this. Appearances were everything.

Everet opened the door and greeted his son with a handshake and a clap on the back. There was no preamble.

"So, you've got problems. About time you listened to your old man, Rollie. What I'd like to know is why you didn't use your experience at the Capitol to better advantage. My guy at the meeting told me you tried to force your way instead of persuading. Force is overrated, Rollie. It's as though you've never watched me and figured out how I'm successful."

"I thought it was a no-brainer, Dad. These people are hicks."

"It looks like you're the hick, son. Arrogant, as well. Anyway, it's water under the bridge. You still have another candidates meeting and you've also got two weeks to canvass the town. So let's figure out how you're going to get elected mayor."

Rollie sat on the Queen Anne settee. "Maybe me getting elected mayor isn't such a smart thing, Dad. Why don't you just buy the property from the town and be done with it?"

"Rollie, sometimes I wonder. We've been through this before and you still don't get it. The property isn't for sale, right? If you're mayor, you can make things happen. Or is that too much work?"

Rollie seemed to shrink when he heard the words. Wasn't his father on his side? Why didn't he encourage him? Sure, the Capitol riot was a mistake, but it wasn't his fault. Rollie looked down at his pudgy hands, his face expressionless.

"I saved you, Rollie. If I hadn't got you into Canada, you'd be rotting in some US jail right now. Enough of the 'it's not my fault' crap. Now's the time you do what I tell you to do. Enough of your crazy ideas. We're now going with what will work."

"You didn't answer my question, Dad."

"OK. Let's start at the beginning. We need to buy the vacant lot near the town hall. It's owned by the town and they think it's worth five million. We want to pay two million. Got that?"

Rollie looked up and nodded. "You've never told me why you don't want to pay the asking price or near it, Dad."

"You don't need to know. Just become mayor and make it happen. Only the mayor can do that. You're a born politician, Rollie. You just don't know it."

Rollie's eyes brightened, hearing a compliment from his father. He looked directly at Everet.

"Yeah, sure. I understand. But how do I get to be mayor? Those councillors jumped on me at the last meeting. Everyone knows and likes them. I'm the newcomer, the stranger."

"You don't have to be, Rollie. Here's what you're going to do."

Rollie always admired his father for his appearance and his way with words. Now he was exposed to Everet's way of thinking. Rollie listened closely.

"Remember these when you're campaigning, Rollie. Repeat them as many times as you can. Everyone suspects politicians are crooked. Think of everything you can accuse the present councillors of doing. Graft, sex with young girls, drunkenness, slamming gay people, cutting down trees. Everet was in full swing now. The list appeared endless.

"But isn't that illegal, Dad?" said Rollie, after an hour of listening to Everet.

"It's only illegal if you get caught, son. Anyway, most people love a good story and they really, really love it if it reinforces their own thinking. Anyway, is there anyone who knows what the truth is?"

"I guess not, Dad," said Rollie. Everet could hear a note of apprehensiveness creeping into Rollie's voice.

"Here's the actual truth. If you keep on repeating something, people will gradually believe it. If you say it enough times, people will think it's their idea. When they reach that point, it's no longer conversation or rumour, it's fact. It's the truth, Rollie. Believe me, I've used it for years."

"Even with your current associates, those guys from Syracuse?"

"Yeah, even them. They think I walk on water, and this investment opportunity in Port Detour is exactly what they need. There's more money coming our way after we pull this one off. Are you OK now, tiger?"

Rollie jumped to his feet and did a fist pump. "Ready to go, Dad."

Chapter 19

"Yeah, thanks. Goodbye," said Dakari to the recorded wake-up call.

His bedside clock showed seven. Standing under the hot running water of the shower muted the shock of rising at such an early hour, and his thoughts turned to the plan for the day. The aim hadn't changed. They needed to find out more information about Kendrick's lost forty years. What might be buried in forty years of isolation from his hometown? Did it even matter? How would they recognize how it might affect the Blue Duck Tavern?

There was one slight problem, one he wished he had asked about before their departure from Port Detour. Now that he thought more about it, there were two problems. Oh well, he could ask when they were back on the road.

He dressed, picked up his carry-on bag, and stumbled into the small dining room of the Northern Gates Motel. His three travelling companions waved to him from their table. As he approached them, he pointed a finger at the group and asked, "Who told the desk to give me a wake up call at seven? I thought we had agreed upon ten?"

"Not me," said each person. Gail added, "Hurry and eat, Dakari. We're raring to go."

He chose some fruit and a coffee from the buffet, ate quickly, standing up, and followed the group to the parking lot. As they neared the van, Rey Rey announced, "I'll drive. I have the directions to Walmart and we can also stop by the Police station and ask about Kendrick." The other three breathed a sigh of relief.

Dakari ignored Rey Rey's words, opened the driver's door, and said, "It's OK, I like to drive." He looked at Rey Rey and Forest. "Remember before we left Port Detour? You two said you didn't like driving, least of all this tank. Anyway, you need to get out at the police station, Rey Rey."

The relaxed looks disappeared, replaced by frowns and tension creases around their mouths. An accident waiting to happen, thought Rey Rey.

Dakari navigated the van onto the street, not checking for any oncoming traffic, and turned to speak to the others. "Does anyone think we just might have made a mistake coming on this wild goose chase? Is this the best way to find out what Kendrick really did over the last forty years? Does anyone here really think he made a living selling bikini swimsuits for a living?"

Dakari's artistic bent of mind was in full view. "Kendrick had to be involved in all sorts of ventures. All illegal, I bet. Imagine the possibilities. He travels from town to town, his place of business is mobile, here today, gone tomorrow, and people can only find him if he tells them where, otherwise they can't find him. I think Kendrick has fed us a bunch of bullshit. Bikini sales, my ass."

Rey Rey got more excited as Dakari spoke. "I know, I know. He was running drugs. Maybe even guns. Maybe a mobile whorehouse."

"What do you think, Gail?" he asked.

"Could be, Rey Rey, could be. Remember two years ago? That private investigator trying to find out all about Kendrick?"

"I remember something, but it was Marg who talked to him and, I guess, you. What did he want?"

"We never found out, Rey Rey. We didn't give him much because we knew little."

Gail added, "Does anybody remember what he was most interested in?"

Everyone shook their head, except Forest.

"I do. Marg told me he wanted to know if Kendrick had any affairs or involvement with women. What a silly question. Of course he did. He's been married four times. Kendrick and his big mouth let everyone know that. He's actually proud of it."

From his tone of voice, the group could hear Forest's disapproval, or maybe envy.

"Anyway, Marg said she didn't think it was important. Something about one of his exes needing information for an alimony claim. Nothing about his business or how he gained his money. She didn't think any of the info was enough not to hire him. Remember, we were kind of desperate because we had little money for an employee."

"Here's a thought worth repeating," said Gail. "Don't you think he may owe a lot of back alimony to those exes of his? The guy's broke. Maybe he's stealing from the tavern."

They all looked at each other. "No way," said Rey Rey, as if Kendrick's character wouldn't permit this. No one else shook their head. It was possible.

Dakari had been silent for the whole speculative conversation. "I know what he did. It's perfect. He's a professional hit man."

Forest's eyes widened. "You mean we hired a murderer?" The impact of that statement dawned on him. "Do you realize what he'll do to us if it's true, and he finds out?"

Dakari couldn't resist. "Yeah Forest, maybe we should all pack some heat."

"Heat? What on earth are you talking about, Dakari? The guy is going to kill us."

Gail was the first to speak. "Dakari, stop baiting him. It's not funny."

Dakari loved intrigue and added, "Don't be so quick to dismiss it. Stranger things have happened. Look at the Enwright twins last year." Everyone nodded their heads, remembering the plot last year to poison one of their members.

"Get real, guys," Gail added. "Does anyone think Kendrick is smart enough to be a hit man, much less do anything else illegal?"

She looked at the group. "We've got work today. Did you know Sudbury has three times the people as North Bay? We'll find someone who knew Kendrick."

Dakari had his own thoughts. What are the odds that one of Kendrick's customers would see the travelling bikini store in an area twice the size of France? When they decided to make the journey, it had sounded oh so exciting and a lot of fun. Visions of an Agatha Christie novel appeared in their mind's eye, amateurs in hot pursuit of a prey.

Dakari wanted more.

"OK. Let's talk about what we'll ask if we find a customer in Sudbury."

There was no comment. The other three investigators continued to look out the windows. Now there was complete silence except for the occasional "Oh, look at that," as they passed a point of interest.

Dakari, after thirty minutes had passed, was bored.

"Maybe he's broke and has robbed as much as he can in Northern Ontario, and now he's robbing the tavern. We should find out if there are any outstanding warrants for his arrest."

"Get real, Dakari. We know he's still walking around, free," said Gail.

Within two hours, the bare rocks around Sudbury appeared. Fifteen minutes later, the van was parked in the middle of the Walmart parking lot, ready for business.

Rey Rey allocated shift times, and the search for any information about Kendrick began. Rey Rey made use of his time by taking a taxi to the police station, but all he got was a promise to phone back if they heard anything.

Back at the van, no one showed up looking for the proprietor of the van, nor had the police phoned back. It made for a long day. One child, in the morning, had passed the van and asked his mother, "Why doesn't that lady have any clothes on?"

Two breaks came late in the afternoon. A woman drove up to the van, got out, pointed to the van, and asked if Kenny was inside.

"Nobody named Kenny is here," replied Gail. "What's your name? Were you maybe looking for Kendrick?"

"No, I'm looking for Kenny," she replied. "I'm Wanda and my daughter's name is Melody. Melody Chordwell. I haven't seen him in over two years. Do you know where he is?"

"Why do you want to see him?" asked Gail.

"The bastard owes my daughter alimony money. Nothing but a con man. Is he here or not?"

"Not right now," said Rey Rey. "If you could tell us more, we'll let him know you need to see him."

"Nothing to tell. We want the money he owes." She pointed a long, tattooed arm at Rey Rey. "When you turn over the rock he's under, let him know Wanda is involved now. He'll know what that means.

Nobody screws my daughter without paying." After a long stare, she finally gave up and drove off in her battered Toyota pickup.

"Well, at least we found out something," said Gail. "It appears Kendrick found it more convenient using another name. But why?"

The second break came around four in the afternoon. An obviously inebriated middle aged man came up to the group sitting around the collapsible table, looked at the bikini-clad starlet on the side of the van and asked Forest what the rate was.

After he left, Rey Rey made a suggestion. "Let's pack up and get out of here. Kendrick appears to be a ghost. We can make the eight PM ferry to Tobermory if we leave now."

"Tobermory? Why Tobermory? Port Detour is south, not west," stated Dakari.

Rey Rey had a surprised look on his face. "Where have you been, Dakari? Going through Tobermory is the shortest way home. That's where the ferry is, the one to Southern Ontario. And it's a beautiful trip, amazing scenery."

"Yeah, I bet, especially at night," said Dakari sarcastically. "How does the captain know where he is? Are there street lights along the way? Probably more rocks, right?"

The three of them ignored his snarky concerns and quickly stowed their gear in the van. The three-hour drive to South Baymouth on Manitoulin Island seemed to take days as far as the passengers could determine. Talk was minimal as reality settled in.

"How did we let ourselves be sucked in?" questioned Forest. "Even if we were to find out Kendrick was an axe murderer, what difference would it make? Well, maybe not an axe murder, but you know what I mean."

Gail spoke up. "I'm sorry for this, everyone. It was my idea, and it looks like a lost cause. I should have known better."

Everyone looked at her but no one said, "It's OK, we understand." They were all complicit. It had been a joint decision. Everyone of them was caught up in the excitement of a chase, all logic thrown out the window.

Just as the sun was starting its descent into the western horizon, they crested a hill and gazed out at a panorama of water, forested hills, small islands and golden water. The road dipped down and ended at the entrance to a long dock extending into the bay. As they drove on to the dock, several male bystanders pointed to the image on the van and tried to peer into the interior to see if it indeed held bikini-clad starlets.

The end of the dock was overshadowed by the raised white bow of a large ship, decorated with a monstrous mural highlighted by a soaring eagle, a wigwam, and a stylized eagle feather. The bow swallowed a stream of vehicles traversing the loading ramp. Their van was the last vehicle on board. The bow started its slow descent to water level, making the ferry look like it was seaworthy again.

A small crowd gathered to view the sunset from the second deck stern. The van and its painted sides could easily be seen. One person in particular, a portly man wearing a Blue Jays ball cap, blue denim shirt and red suspenders, seemed over the top excited.

"Hey Kenny. It's me," He waved furiously. "Up here. I'm coming down."

Within thirty seconds, he appeared on the vehicle deck and ran full tilt towards the bikini-clad starlet. He reached the driver's door and pulled it open.

"Kenny. Kenny Rogers. Is that you? I haven't seen you for years. How are you, man?"

"Sir, sir, stop" said Rey Rey, shrinking to the farthest edge of the driver's seat.

"Oh, I'm sorry. I thought you were Kenny," said the heavily breathing man. "Why have you got Kenny's truck? Did he sell it?"

Suddenly, Dakari's hand clapped Rey Rey on the shoulder and he whispered in his ear, "Don't tell him a thing."

Rey Rey didn't, answering in a non-committal way.

"Not quite, sir. We're good friends of Kenny. We're from Port Detour and he lent us the van for a fishing trip. How do you know him?"

"Know him? He was my neighbour and buddy for the past thirty years. And I know where Port Detour is because he moved there over two years ago. I haven't heard from him since."

"Well, he's now a good friend of ours. What did you say your name is?"

"I didn't, but it's Floyd, Floyd Waters. How about that? Running into friends of Kenny. C'mon, we gotta have a drink and you can bring me up to date about our buddy. Ya know, it's strange. He asked me to take care of the place until he sold it. Never heard a peep from him after he moved away. Did you keep in touch when he lived in Sudbury?"

"Not really," said Dakari. "He said little about his time there. We'd love to hear more. Let's go for that drink. We got two hours until we land, right?"

Dakari got out of the van, grabbed Floyd's arm and steered him to the stairs leading up to the second floor cafeteria. He let him go first and as the other three passed by, he said, "Play along. I bet he knows everything about Kendrick.

"Ooh, I love this," said Gail, suddenly released from Ancient History.

Dakari asked everyone what they wanted to drink and returned from the bar area with five beers and four bags of BBQ flavoured chips.

"Kenny is a great guy," said Floyd. "Life of the party. Never at a loss for words. And he was smart. Knew everything. How do you guys know him?"

"He's now the bartender at our club. The Blue Duck," said Dakari.

"I knew it, I knew it," exclaimed Floyd. "That guy can't sit still for a second. Always had to do something. You know, he said he made a fortune in real estate. He just ran that van for fun. He could charm the …'" He paused, "Sorry, there are ladies present. I'll shut up." He farted, let go a big laugh, and downed his beer.

For the next two hours, the Blue Duck delegation was treated to tales about Kenny and his exploits.

"Do you know he told me everything? We were brothers. Couldn't believe half what he said, but boy, was he entertaining. Liked the ladies too, and they just fell all over him. Married four times."

He laughed at the thought. "Couldn't afford them, though. Big time alimony payments, he told me. But he never told me where he got his money. Probably illegal, knowing him. He could talk a rattlesnake out of its skin."

A half hour away from their destination, Floyd grew serious. "Ya know he had his share of troubles?"

"No, not really. He's always put on a good face with us," said Gail. "Tell us more."

It was a monologue. Floyd talked. Dakari, Rey Rey, Gail and Forest listened. Floyd also added his own editorial comments, especially about the first three wives. Apparently, Kendrick was a better lover than a negotiator. Other than wife number one, the next two wives won large financial settlements, something he bitterly complained about to anyone who would listen.

"What about wife number one?" asked Gail. "Wasn't she on the gravy train, also?"

"Kendrick wouldn't talk about that. Joanne was her name. Joanne Bilocki, from French River. I didn't know her, but I met some people who did, people who knew Kendrick in his younger days. They told me she just disappeared. Big mystery."

"Could she have met a mysterious death, Floyd?" asked Dakari.

Forest's fears were confirmed. "I knew it, I knew it. Dakari, you were right. Kendrick is a murderer. A cold-blooded murderer. We should let the police know."

Gail was alarmed. "Stop it, Forest. Floyd, ignore him. He's got this bee in his bonnet about Kendrick. We know nothing. And Dakari, stop riling up Forest. He'll have a heart attack if you keep this up."

Floyd's answer was of no help. "I don't know, guys. Anyway, three years ago, Kendrick announced he was moving to Port Detour. I don't know why, but he still owned the tiny bungalow in the development next door to me. Big problem. Even at the price Kendrick wanted, no one showed any interest in buying or even renting. It's still vacant."

Floyd looked around at the surrounding landscape, now almost completely dark. The lights of the ferry terminal glowed a mile away, like a star in a night sky.

"We're here, folks. What luck running into you. I'm glad Kenny is back on his feet. He's had some tough years. Anybody else would have become a drunk. On top of that, between you and me, I think he lost all his money. Take care of him for me and make sure you tell him you ran into Floyd."

With that, he was gone, leaving four people sitting around the table looking at each other with wide eyes.

"Time to get back to the van, people. We can discuss this on the way. I'm not sure we heard the complete story, though," said Dakari. "We still don't know how he could afford the alimony payments. Where did the money come from?"

As they rose, Dakari added. "I still like my theory. A hit man."

Chapter 20

Rey Rey, Forest, Dakari and Gail piled into the van, Dakari in the driver's seat with no objection from his passengers. As his driving competence increased, so did their confidence in making him the assigned driver.

They looked at each other for a moment and then Dakari asked, "Who wants to start?"

Gail was the first to speak. "It's exactly what I would have expected from Kendrick. We learned nothing that was a surprise and we certainly haven't found out how he earned a living. Even his buddy Floyd didn't know. I'm stumped. What now?"

Dakari's kufu bobbed up and down in agreement and he started the engine. The long line of cars ahead of him moved, and five minutes later, they cleared the exit ramp.

"There it is," pointed Forest from the passenger seat. The road marker said Owen Sound and underneath it, Toronto. "Follow that road, Dakari."

Gail spoke from the back seat. "According to my phone map, it's going to take us over six hours to get to Port Detour. It's midnight now, so what's everyone want to do? Drive through or stay in a motel?"

"Let's drive through," said Forest. Every head nodded in agreement. "Are you OK with driving, Dakari?"

"No problem, Forest. I'm a night owl. Anyway, I'm getting some splendid views of the forest. I've already got three ideas for the future." The group was so tired they buried any fears they had about Dakari's driving competence and all nodded OK.

Rey Rey picked up the conversation. "Yeah, what did he do? Anybody want to talk about what we heard tonight?" asked Rey Rey.

"Tomorrow," said Gail, "I'm half asleep. I'm going to close my eyes for a bit." No one else objected, and the van was soon quiet, other than the sound of the motor and what sounded like a broken muffler. Gail snored. Dakari was left alone with his thoughts, trying to make sense of what they had heard from Floyd. None of the things they had speculated about had risen. How could so much be hidden for so long? It was very complicated, what with women, wives and money. Not that it bothered him. His last forty years were a parallel universe.

The long drive also generated recurring questions in every person's mind. Why had Kendrick left Port Detour, and why had he returned?

At six o'clock, the sun came up directly in Dakari's face, flooding the van with light. The passengers gradually roused.

"How's it going, Dakari? Still on the road I see," said Rey Rey.

He allowed himself one joke. "Why are we heading west to Detroit, Dakari? Are you lost?"

Dakari spun around, completely ignoring the road. "What do you mean, Rey Rey? We're heading in the right direction." He added, "Aren't we?"

Rey Rey laughed, "It's OK, Dakari. You're doing great. The sun rises in the East. Just follow it home. Only another thirty minutes and we'll be there. Hey everyone, what should we do with our newfound info?"

"We should publish it in the Port Detour Times," said Dakari.

"No way," replied Rey Rey, astonishment on his face. "We can't do that." A frown showed on his face as he recognized Dakari was only giving back what he, Rey Rey, had dished out.

Gail had already analyzed the problem. "We need to get together with Marg and Emile before we do anything. Maybe they have info as well. Forest, why don't you phone Marg and find out where they are and what they've found?"

Just at that moment, they turned on to the exit to Port Detour. Forest didn't make the call. He was entranced by what he saw.

"Rey Rey, Dakari, Gail, look at that." He pointed to an enormous billboard at the end of the exit. The headline read, 'Let's Take Our Town Back. Get Rid Of Corrupt Councillors'. Underneath these words was a notice. 'Attend the All Candidates meeting October 10 at 4 PM. Let's elect people who know how to take care of our money, not spend it on themselves.'

The name of the sponsoring organization at the bottom read '*The Committee For Fair and Responsible Government. Rollie Overland, President.*'

"My God, I forgot the election is next week," said Gail. "Anybody want to go to that meeting?"

"Boring, Gail." said Dakari. "I'll pass. More boring political promises with no action. I think I'll clean my painting brushes that night."

"Hilarious, Dakari, only it's not funny. Nobody knows why Rollie Overland is running for mayor."

"Why do we care?" asked Rey Rey.

Gail looked like she might pounce on him. "Because Mr. Smartass, he's Everet's son and Kendrick's nephew. Doesn't that generate a little concern, or have you been living among the dead too long?"

"No need to get nasty, Gail. Perhaps we should attend the meeting."

Chapter 21

Kendrick pounced on the ringing phone, pushing aside the remnants of his evening meal. The call display showed the name E. Overland.

He punched the answer button and said 'Kendrick Overland' in as casual a tone as possible. His heart was racing. Not that he wanted Everet to know.

"Hey bro, the deal's confirmed. We're all go, so put the wheels in motion like we discussed."

"That's great, Everet. Anything else I need to know?"

"One thing. My client squeezed me some more. Now I gotta do some other things like get permits, environmental approval and a bunch of other approvals from the town planning department. It's gonna cost me. You'll have to take a lower share. OK?"

Under his breath, Kendrick had called Everet a bastard the last time they talked. Now he raised the level to blood sucker. "How much, Everet?"

"Not much of a change, bro. It's now sixty-five, thirty-five."

"If I have a choice, Everet, I liked the last deal. Sixty, forty."

"Sorry, you don't have a choice. Anyway, it's still a whack of money. Don't complain."

The connection disappeared from his phone.

Chapter 22

Marg slept soundly and woke just before seven. She was surprised, and pleased, given she had a room-mate, and a man to boot. Her cell phone rang, and she glanced over at Emile's bed.

Emile sat up, gave Marg an annoyed look, decided he wasn't interested in overhearing the conversation, and made his way to the bathroom for his morning cleanup. It was seven o'clock.

"Hello? Who's this?" said Marg weakly, still groggy from sleep. "Oh, hi Kendrick, what do you want at this hour of the morning? Hopefully, you're not having a drink at the tavern." There was silence as she listened to Kendrick.

Then, "So you got the OK."

More silence as Marg listened to whatever Kendrick was telling her.

She forced herself to say the next logical reply. "What do you need?"

"Hang on a minute, Kendrick. I have to take some notes so I'll turn on my speaker. OK. go ahead."

Kendrick continued. "Everet's client is going to send a substantial amount of money to him. He'll use it to buy a building site for their new Canadian operation."

"Yes, you told me that last time we spoke. Everet doesn't want to be identified with this transaction. He wants you to hold the money until it's needed and then you disburse it according to his instructions. Strange behaviour on his part, isn't it?"

"It's a little more complicated. Everet can't do business in Canada since he's got a criminal record. You knew that, right?"

"I've heard rumours, Kendrick. So, he wants you to set up a company to receive and disburse the money. You're the front, right?"

"No, no. I don't want anyone to know I have the money. My ex-wives would pounce on that like fleas on a dog. I probably forgot to tell you, but I owe a bit of back alimony."

"What a surprise, Kendrick. How much?"

"You understand it's two of my four wives? They were the worst blood, no, make that money suckers, I've ever seen. And I might have boasted a bit about how wealthy I am, so they went for the kill. It's not peanuts. It's in the hundreds of thousands."

Marg was silent for a moment. "Some of that's new info, Kendrick, some isn't. What you need is a numbered private company. Those types of companies aren't required to show who owns them."

"Numbered company?" asked Kendrick.

"Yes, Kendrick. They do not differ from any other company, but instead of someone having to dream up a name, it's assigned a number by the government. And the owner doesn't have to be named."

"That's what we need. Charge ahead."

"But what about Everet? Isn't he going to want some legal agreement between you and him?"

"Like I said, Marg, he can't be associated with a company in Ontario. Our agreement will be a handshake. That's all he needs."

"When do you need this? Today?" she asked with a laugh.

"Yeah, I do. Can you do it?"

"Sure. I can have it done. Like I told you, we'll need to involve another lawyer." On second thought, she added, "and it'll cost a lot of money, Kendrick."

"No problem. Just take it out of the money coming in today. It's around five mill."

What a bullshitter, thought Marg. The way he said 'five mill' made it sound like this was petty cash. "I'll call you with the details later today. What bank do you want to use?"

"Use the Commerce & Savings Bank Marg. They don't know me there."

"Yeah, I can do that, Kendrick. As I said to you last time, it'll be one of my legal friends in Toronto, so be prepared to supply an arm and a leg. I gotta go. You'll hear from my friend later today. Let me know how it goes. Goodbye."

Emile returned from the washroom. "What's that about? Got another man on the side, Marg?"

"Not funny, Emile. It was Kendrick. Let's get going. I can hardly wait to find out what your bulldog friend Spike has found out. How did he get that name, anyway?"

"Just a nickname, Marg. Within the FBI he's known to never give up. Just like a bulldog's bite. Tough guy." Marg wondered if Emile wasn't talking about himself. After all, likes attract. Hopefully, she was in the same space as Spike.

Chapter 23

Marg settled the bill at the front desk. "I'll drive, Emile, since you've got to get out and meet Spike." She found the car, and they picked up their breakfast at a McDonald's drive-through. Ten minutes later, following the GPS, she pulled up in front of an ugly grey government building. The sign said FBI.

"Marg, wait for me here. You need a pass to get in and also be a law enforcement official. Spike has arranged it and I'm going to meet him at his office and see what he's got. Sorry about that."

Emile got out and stuck his head back in the car.. "I don't think I'll be long. Wait right here. No need to park." Then he was off to the front doors.

Marg pulled out her phone and made a call to Toronto. "Hi Anne, I need a favour." She explained what her client, Kendrick, needed to her friend, received assurance it would be done, and then hung up.

Bored, she tuned the radio to the local station and listened for a few minutes about the latest convenience store robbery, a fire on the east side of town and the town council's debate about the homeless encampment.

Within five minutes, the driver's door opened and Emile said, "Got it, Marg," and handed her a thick brown manila envelope, unaddressed.

"Why don't you let me drive while you look over what we have? You know Everet and his brother better than I do, so it may mean more to you." Marg moved over to the passenger side and Emile settled behind the wheel.

"Go on, open it. Spike said he has given us copies of everything he found. I didn't look since Spike wanted me in and out real quick before anyone saw us. Must be hot material."

Emile put the car in gear, took a quick glance at Marg, and pulled away for the curb. "Well? Can we go home? Have we got what we need?"

"Give me a moment, Emile. Wow, you are impatient. Keep driving while I go through this stuff. There's a lot here."

She extracted the contents and sorted them into two piles on her lap. One pile comprised what appeared to be transcripts of conversations. The other pile were photographs, long distance surveillance shots mostly, and a few shots from police lineups. There was a single page memo on top.

"Well? what does Spike say?"

"Emile, just keep driving. The memo is dated yesterday. Let me read it to you."

Marg took the sheet and perused it for a moment. "Wow, organized crime. Then he says not to tell anybody where we got the info."

She was silent for a minute. "New York and Syracruse, Emile. This is big time crime. He says that until a few years ago, Everet was accused several times of defrauding at least five women of their life savings. He was only convicted once and spent one year in jail. Since then, no mention of women."

"That's all?"

"No, that's not all, but it's kind of important to the women who were defrauded, Emile. You've been a cop too long. You're jaded. But his last comment is the interesting, one. In fact, it's startling."

"So tell me. What could a loser like Everet possibly do that's worse than robbing old ladies?"

"Did anyone ever teach you patience, Emile?"

"Are you going to let me know, or do I have to torture you?" Emile briefly took his eyes off the road to stare at Marg.

Marg flipped through the pile of paper and photos. "It's here, Emile. Our buddy Everet isn't a two-bit criminal. He's playing in the big leagues. There are all kinds of handwritten notes on the photographs showing Everet with, I guess, some known organized crime and even Mafia characters. Wow, look at this." She held up a single printed page, single spaced.

Emile tried to take a quick glance at the page and almost drove off the road. He slowed down, pulled over to the side and grabbed the paper from Marg's hand.

"Money laundering? He's the mob money laundering guy in Syracuse? Marg, I'm not sure what we've stumbled across, but we're not dealing with some petty larceny here. Everet's in Port Detour for a reason, and it probably involves Kendrick and even the Blue Duck. We should also include Rollie. Why is he tagging along?"

"Emile, this is only half of what's happening. Let's get back to Port Detour and see what the other group has found out about Kendrick. Maybe they aren't the fighting Overlands so much as the 'in cahoots' Overlands."

Emile put the car back in gear and gunned it back on the expressway.

Chapter 24

Marg's cell phone rang. She looked at the call display and pressed 'speaker'.

"Hi Forest, how's your investigation going?"

"And good day to you, Marg. Where are you?"

"We're on our way back from Syracuse. We'll be back in Port Detour around three o'clock. Why do you ask? Did you find anything about Kendrick? Was your trip a success?"

Forest decided to lie. How else would he justify the time and trouble they incurred? "Marg, you won't believe what we found. What about you and Emile? Have you found anything of interest about Everet?"

"Yeah, a little," she answered casually, winking at Emile. "We'll fill you and the others in when we see you. But why did you call? "

She wasn't inclined to be more open with Forest until her brain had processed the latest information about Everet. Also, not being able to see Forest's face was a problem. Who knew what her literal minded friend would make of the words 'organized crime?'. Her voice assumed a harsh, unwelcome tone. Forest appeared not to notice.

"It's about the election, Marg. Rollie's gone wild. You should hear what he's saying about the councillors. I'll be surprised if he won't be sued for libel. Maybe he will, but I wanted to remind you and Emile that there's the all-candidates meeting this evening. Rollie will be there, as well as all the other candidates. We should all be there."

"We'll be back in plenty of time. See you there."

Chapter 25

Emile looked over at Marg in the passenger seat and said nothing. Marg frowned, "What is it, Emile? Did I sprout another head?"

"Marg, do you realize that this arrangement with Kendrick must have to do with money laundering? Kendrick is in way over his head. Not only that, these associates of Everet's play for keeps. If anything goes wrong with whatever arrangements they have concocted, somebody is going to get hurt. Maybe dead. We've got to do some thinking here."

Marg thought for a moment. "But right now we have got nothing solid. No money has moved, nor has there been any attempt to set up a laundering scheme. Don't you think we should let it play out a bit more before we take action?"

Emile concentrated on driving. Marg could see him tapping the wheel, trying to work out what should be done. Swirling around in his mind were conflicting thoughts. Sure, he wasn't in law enforcement anymore, but the training and habits of a lifetime in the field were hard to ignore. If he were still in the force, he would be on the phone in seconds. Now he was dealing with friends. Well, Kendrick wasn't a friend, more like the proverbial lamb being sent to slaughter.

"All right," he finally said, taking a quick look at her. "Let's leave it until we see what unfolds."

Hours passed with innocuous chit chat and listening to the top forty gospel songs on CGOD, The Voice of God In The Country. They were in a dead spot. Nothing else was available. After listening to forecasts of doom and gloom and the fires of hell for an hour, they turned off the radio and rode in silence for the next three hours. They arrived in Port Detour in plenty of time to attend the rally. At Marg's request, they made a brief stop at the Commerce Bank.

"Just double park, Emile. I won't be long," she said as she got out. Entering the bank, she asked to see the manager and waited a few minutes until he showed up.

"How can I help you?" he asked. Marg explained she needed to arrange banking for a new company she owned and all the legal papers had been couriered over to the bank earlier in the day. She needed to have the bank arrangements done immediately, which prompted a protest from Freddie Gold in his capacity as manager. It wouldn't be appropriate for a customer to demand anything from a bank, thought Freddie. Next, they would ask for personal service.

"How much will the initial deposit be, Ms. O'Toole?" asked Freddy.

"I believe it is around five million, Mr. Gold."

Freddie had second thoughts. A real customer. "Come with me, Ms. O'Toole. We can use my office."

"Please make it as fast as possible, Mr. Gold. My car is waiting outside." The papers, including the signature card, were presented and signed within five minutes. Freddie Gold tried to make conversation, unsuccessfully, which only proved to him he was now dealing with a very important new account. Marg received a welcome kit and account details, shook Freddie's hand, exited the front doors and took a few steps to the passenger side of Emile's car.

"All set, Marg?" asked Emile.

"Couldn't be more perfect, Emile. We're set."

Emile put the car in gear, drove away from the no-parking zone and glanced at Marg. She had a slight smile on her face and turned to face him.

She repeated herself. "Yes Emile, we're really set. It's surprising how things have turned out. Stick around, it's going to get even better."

Chapter 26

Three of the Blue Duck members had front row seats in a standing room only crowd at the Port Detour Legion Hall. The three had arrived early, mistakenly thinking the event started at six, their sense of time distorted by their near sleepless night travelling. Dakari was absent, and they laid claim to a seat for him and also two for Emile and Marg, who arrived five minutes before the event started. Dakari showed up at the last moment, completely out of breath.

"It's a long way from the bus stop to here," he said to no one in particular. "I've been on the phone for forty minutes and had to run from the bus to here."

Rey Rey looked startled. "Dakari, it's only fifty metres, and it's level. Don't you ever exercise?"

"No. Why would I?"

Rey Rey let it lie. He turned to Marg.

"What did you find out, Marg? Is he just a common criminal?"

"Nothing common about Everet, Rey Rey," said Marg. "We hit the jackpot with that one."

Everyone leaned forward, trying to hear what the jackpot might be. Forest, his voice muted, said, "Jackpot? What do you mean?"

His question went unanswered as Ricky Walton approached the lectern, looked at the crowd and then at the candidates flanking the podium. Yogi Berra's often repeated remark crossed his thoughts,

'It's deja vu all over again'. The same candidates, sitting in the same places on stage as last time with the same audience and the same coloured walls. Both the high school and the Legion must have used the same painter using the same paint - a sickly olive green colour.

Like the paint, no doubt the same promises would be made again tonight. That was a problem, but he had an idea.

"OK folks, let's get going. You know the format, but I'd like to point out that this second 'meet the candidate' meeting is meant to hear new thoughts from our candidates. We don't want to hear a repeat of what we heard last meeting."

"We also have one change to our format. We'll entertain questions from the audience at the end of each person's talk."

He paused before continuing. The audience quieted.

"There's one other thing. Our Mayor declined to attend this meeting and no one, other than Rollie Overland, put their name down for the position. So we'll let our mayoral candidate go first."

That should set the bar, Ricky thought. What he'd heard over the last two weeks, when interviewing a cross section of residents, were the most exciting comments and accusations he had ever heard in Port Detour. Graft, theft, favouritism and plain old nepotism were the mainstay of gossip at the local coffee shops and bars. Rollie, while canvassing, claimed he had the evidence. The citizens of Port Detour loved it. They were vindicated. Rollie's 'facts' proved their suspicions were correct.

Gert and Lydia sat beside each other in the front row. "This is so exciting, Lydia," said Gert, looking back over the packed meeting room. "That young man, Rollie, is Everet's son. You remember him - we met at the Blue Duck Club a few weeks back."

"So that's who he is," replied Lydia. "I thought I recognized him. He's got his father's looks and the gift of the gab. I'll vote for him. From what I hear, he's going to shake up the town if he's elected. Did you hear what he told Charley Valance?"

"No. Why would he tell anything to Charley? That old coot's almost senile."

"He didn't just tell Charlie, Gert. Everyone has been told. He says all our councillors are on the take and he has proof. Not only that, all those cushy jobs only go to their relatives. That I know for a fact. Just look at the people Homer hires. Everyone in the Works Department is related to Homer."

"My gosh, you're right, Gert. Anything else?"

They were interrupted by Rollie, who got up and went to the lectern, carrying a brown manila file folder. He pulled the mic from the stand and moved around to stand in front of the lectern. His hands shook, and he planted his feet wide apart. His voice assumed a high pitch, and he almost shouted.

"I get riled up just thinking about what the mayor and his councillors have done to us, and so should you."

"I'm the new kid in town, and I want to be your mayor. Why? Because we shouldn't have to put up with any more nepotism, money mismanagement and shoddy services." His voice changed, and he shouted, "And high taxes Enough is enough."

"Elect me and my team." he swept his arm toward the right and motioned for each person to stand. "Here's what you will get - fresh thinking and integrity." He then moved his hand down, much like one does to quiet a jumping dog. They sat down in unison.

"Everyone of these people," he pointed at each of the incumbent councillors, "have lined their pockets and you've paid for it with high taxes."

He paused and raised the envelope. "I have it right here, in black and white. Let me tell you, if I give this to the police right now, this town wouldn't have a mayor and councillors. Sorry, a correction. You would still have councillors and a mayor, but after their name, the words 'convicted criminal' would appear."

Stunned silence ensued.

"Let's move on. People often ask me, what makes a young guy like you qualified to be mayor?"

He looked around the room as if he was the one making the enquiry.

"Good question. I have been involved in politics my entire adult life, starting with being Student Union President at university. After graduating, I worked on campaigns for several state politicians and finally I was the right-hand man for the governor of the state I just came from."

Ricky was furiously taking notes. His last entry was, 'no one seemed to object to the wild claims made by Rollie'. It had taken a while, but Councillor Brady, seated to the left of the podium, jumped up as if a spring in his chair had poked through the seat cover. He pointed his finger at Rollie and yelled.

"All this is nonsense. None of us take bribes. We work hard to make sure our town is run properly, and for the taxpayers. This is nothing but lies."

Rollie raised the file folder above his head. "It's right here, sir. All in black and white." He looked at the councilmen and said. "This is a police matter. I'm turning all this evidence over to the police. I'm sure you and the other councilmen will hear from them shortly."

He then laughed. "Unless you've paid them off."

That was the trigger. The other councilmen moved from their chairs and surrounded Rollie. Fists were raised, and a punch was thrown by a councillor. Ricky went down, the target of an errant fist.

After five minutes of tussling and the arrival of the police, Rollie held up his arm and yelled, "Remember, voting day is one week away. Please vote for us and let's get Port Detour under your control again. Let's stop the graft and bribery."

The Blue Duck members, seated in the front row, didn't take part in the frenzy, but took it all in. Within thirty minutes, the turmoil subsided, but the event was over. As the attendees streamed out of the Legion, the six Blue Duck members gathered as a group on the front steps.

Rey Rey was the first to speak. "Don't you think he makes sense? Many people, including me, have often wondered if these guys are on the take."

"Can't prove it, though." said Dakari. The others nodded in agreement. "You're the cop Emile. Have you heard any of this before?"

"It's not true, everyone. There are always rumours, but take it from me, nothing of that scale has happened. Maybe a restaurant meal or tickets to the hockey game. But nothing like Rollie is accusing them of. Makes for good vote getting, though."

He added, "It looks like Rollie is grandstanding. I think all he has in the envelope is last week's newspaper."

Forest piped up. "I agree. It's great acting on his part and it certainly appeals to the voters. I feel that Rollie and his pals are going to be elected based on lies. That's a grand project for the Blue Duck Club. What are these guys up to?"

Nobody could add anything to that thought. Forest continued. "We found out some amazing stuff on our trip, but if something is going on with Rollie, Everet and Kendrick, I don't have a clue what it is. Rollie didn't run for mayor just because he's ambitious. So let's wait until we see what he and his running mates do. Maybe, just maybe, what we need to know will be crystal clear in a few weeks. What do you say?"

"I'm not OK with that," said Emile. "For sure there's something going on here. Let's compare what we found on our trips. Then we can decide what to do." Everyone nodded in agreement. "What's a good place to meet?"

"My place, ten o'clock tomorrow morning," said Dakari. "I've got the studio with lots of space and it's private. No one has to know what we're doing, least of all Kendrick and Everet."

Marg stayed silent through the conversation, paying close attention to what was discussed. She frowned as though something wrong had been said. After their meeting had been set, Marg looked around the group. She wasn't smiling and asked, "So we're going to get together, and then what? "

Everyone looked at her. She continued. "Just like your trip north, is it? Did you find out what you wanted because of your plan? In fact, what was your plan?"

"What are you talking about, Marg?" asked Rey Rey. The aggressive statement was not like the Rey Rey his fellow members knew. Forest wondered if retirement had caused Rey Rey to question his role in life. Everyone recognized Rey Rey's next statement as nothing but an exaggeration. "You don't know what we found out, but I guarantee you it'll be an eye-opener. For you especially."

"What's that supposed to mean?" asked Marg with the same intensity as if she were questioning a witness.

Rey Rey didn't back down. "I don't know why you're so critical, Marg. We were successful, as you'll see." He couldn't resist a parting shot. "I doubt even you could have found out the information we got. Maybe our plan didn't work out as well as we hoped, but we got results, and that's what matters. I hope you and Emile got half of what we did."

Marg sensed she might have touched a sore spot and added, "Oh, we got plenty, Rey Rey. But what I'm driving at is how are we going to make sense of the information we've gathered? What's the plan of attack?"

Rey Rey was still smarting and decided that attack was better than being passive. No one in the undertaking business had talked to him like that, and he was unsure he even knew what to do.

"So Marg, how would the big city lawyer handle this?"

"Calm down Rey Rey. I'm sorry I was so abrupt. You don't deserve it. I guess I saw you as the big city prosecutor for a moment."

He smiled, and his face and voice projected confidence. In his eyes, he was now regarded as a person of worth. "Really? Thanks Marg. Anyway, you have more experience than us. How would you approach this?"

Marg again looked around at the group. "It's easy, guys. Emile would know this. He's a cop and has probably analyzed this sort of information dozens of times."

Emile smiled knowingly. "Sure have, Marg." If the group could see inside him, he would have to acknowledge he didn't have a clue what Marg was talking about.

"It's called a Connect The Dots board," said Marg, making it up on the fly.

Everyone nodded knowingly. They had all seen police shows on TV.

"You're right Marg," said Rey Rey. "That's the way to go. Good thinking."

He couldn't think of anything else to add. The TV shows were always light on details. The next thing to pop into his mind brought the gathering to an end with a question.

"Who are you voting for?" he asked.

"What an interesting question," said Gail. "I really don't know. It appears they are all crooks."

Chapter 27

Emile remembered when they were called tree-huggers. The path to Dakari's front door was bordered by the remnants of a lawn, the area choked with weeds. In the middle of this jungle was a large sign saying 'Do Not Weed. This is Natural Native Growth. Preserve Our Environment.' Ironically, he thought, that didn't extend to the Overland brothers.

They knocked, opened the door and walked along the hallway to Dakari's studio at the rear of the house. The walls were completely covered with paintings, sketches, pages from manuscripts. Dakari rounded up some folding chairs and everyone sat down facing a long cork display board along the south wall of the studio. Marg found some coloured sticky-backed notepads and a blue marker.

She turned and faced the others. "OK, you've seen the TV shows where they pin up little tidbits of information and, like magic, the connections are made, the killer is identified and arrested. We're going to do that here. Both Emile and I have some experience in this, so let's get started. Forest, what did you learn about Kendrick?"

"Well, he was married four times, not counting the one on his return to Port Detour."

"So what, Forest? Give us some details."

It was as if Forest completely forgot that Gail, Dakari and Rey Rey were also present when they talked to Floyd. He stared out the window, wanting to be exact in his recall of details.

"We ran into a guy named Floyd Waters, who was Kendrick's neighbour for over twenty years. He and Kendrick were buddies, and Floyd knew a lot about Kendrick's life. Apparently, his ex-wives took him to the cleaners. He owes so much even VISA turned him down."

Marg wrote 'owes a lot of money' on one of the sticky notes and attached it to the board.

It was as if the floodgates had opened. Everyone volunteered information about Kendrick. Five minutes went by and Marg had not added a single fresh note to the bulletin board. She put up her hand and stopped the talking.

"None of this is especially new. All you're doing is repeating some hearsay from a guy name Floyd who, from what you've told me, always has a can of beer in his hand. Have you never heard about asking leading questions from a reputable witness?"

"Right on, Marg," said Dakari. "I could never figure out how touring around Northern Ontario would give us any information about what Kendrick might have done for forty years."

"Rey Rey swung his gaze to Dakari." You suggested no better, Dakari. You're the same as us."

"Not true, Rey Rey. You probably don't understand, having a career like you had."

"Just what's that supposed to mean, Dakari? We had the most successful funeral business in town."

He sat back in his chair and folded his arms, daring anyone to top that evidence.

"What I meant, Rey Rey, is you never had to find out how people died. You just put them six feet under. You were only concerned with the result. I'm an artist and need to know who people are and why they do things. I need to express this in a painting or a sculpture."

"I've no idea what you're talking about, Dakari," responded Rey Rey. "All you need is to listen to people talk. That'll tell you who and what they are."

Dakari looked at Rey Rey as if he were a freak.

"I'm sure none of your clients said a word, Rey Rey. They were all dead. What did that tell you?"

"Stop it, you two," said Marg in a loud voice. "But Rey Rey has a point. What do you know we don't?"

"OK everyone, here's what I did. I thought nothing that Floyd told us was of much use. Even he couldn't explain where Kendrick got his money to live on. So I took action and did my own investigation."

He slowly stood up, his face taking on a serious look, and took a few minutes to look at his fellow members. It also looked like he was enjoying the mystery he had created.

"When we got back, I phoned Floyd and got the names and cell numbers of his neighbours, the ones who would know Kendrick the best. Then I talked to each of them. They were more than willing to share information about Kendrick's life in Sudbury. Kendrick wasn't as well liked as he might imagine." He paused. Everyone nodded in agreement.

"Here's something none of you might know. Kendrick's fourth relationship was common-law. Marie was her name, and she died three years ago. Can you guess what was unusual about that hook up?"

Gail knew. "Kendrick and Marie had a child, a girl. It's not a secret, Dakari."

"Right. She's about eight years old now, but what you may not know is she is severely handicapped. Her name is Sandra. Kendrick has never mentioned this, has he?"

"So where is the girl now?" asked Marg.

"The neighbours didn't know, but the child requires institutional care for her entire life. That's costly, big time."

Marg recorded the information on a card and posted it on the board. Forest provided additional information about Kendrick, including where he lived in Sudbury.

"That's what we found, Marg. What about you and Emile?" asked Gail.

"Wait a minute," said Dakari, still standing in the middle of the group. "I'm not finished."

"Are you telling us you found out how Kendrick made his fortune?" asked Forest.

"He's a bullshitter, Dakari. Why should we believe anything?"

"Because I found out all about his first wife. He married her shortly after he arrived in Sudbury. Anyone want to know what I found? Even Floyd, his best friend, doesn't know this."

"Wait a minute, Dakari. The first wife disappeared. There's talk she is dead, maybe murdered. No one knows what happened."

Marg watched Dakari closely. He was a showman, a free spirit, and it showed. He paused dramatically, almost preening in his multi-coloured robe and hat. Finally, Rey Rey couldn't contain himself.

"Come on, Dakari. What did you find?"

"Kendrick used to be worth a fortune. It happened shortly after he came north and met Joanne Biloki."

"Who's Joanne Biloki?"

"His first wife and also Kendrick's gold mine. They got married, but Kendrick didn't know her family owned mines, construction companies, real estate and more. Rich as Croesus. As a wedding gift, the old man gave the happy couple a subdivision, mostly undeveloped. You can guess the rest."

"What do you mean, Dakari?" asked Forest. "All they needed was a house, not a subdivision."

Dakari had an answer. He added, "After two years they got divorced. Now this is really strange. Somehow, Kendrick got half the assets and a year later, sold it for a fortune. No one saw Joanne again."

"See, I told you," offered Forest. "My good friend is rich."

"Wrong. As Marg once said, all Kendrick has is chutzpah. That and naivete don't mix well. Since he was so rich, he was an attractive catch for the next two wives. They bled him dry. He has nothing. The fourth marriage to Marie was for love. All the money was gone by then."

"So? Was Joanne murdered?" asked Rey Rey. Silence reigned for a good minute until Dakari broke it.

"She moved to Puerto Rico according to her family. She's a recluse. Her family hasn't seen her in years. In fact, they haven't seen her since the divorce. Their only contact with her is an annual letter from her." He added, "Convenient, isn't it?"

Emile looked at Marg. "Ever been to Puerto Rico, Marg?"

"I was thinking the same thing, Emile."

"Keep on topic, Marg," said Forest. "Vacations should be the farthest thing from our minds right now. What about you Marg? And Emile?" he added. "What did you find that tops that?"

"We found plenty, Dakari." She picked up a blank note, wrote 'convicted con artist' on it, and pinned it on the bulletin board.

"I knew it, I knew it," repeated Gail. "There's something about that man that just grates on you."

"That's just a small part of the problem," Emile said. "It's a much larger issue." He paused and looked at Marg. She nodded.

"His MO is remarkably consistent. He hooks up with wealthy divorcees or widows, bleeds them poor, and then moves on to the next victim. He's only been caught once, so he's good at it."

No one said anything. Marg could see the same thing going through everyone's mind. They were now associated with a real criminal. It was one thing to know someone who broke the law, but this? Emile continued.

"His last charge shows a change in career. He was arrested for fraud this time, three years ago, but got off on a technicality. And this wasn't some rich widow he defrauded. This was a business fraud. He's in the big leagues now."

"What do you mean, 'the big leagues'?" asked Forest. He was trying to recall the theft of ten thousand dollars of cash receipts at Smith & Sons, which he had uncovered ten years ago. Was this more than that?

"A couple of million, Forest." revealed Emile. "A bit of violence was also involved. That's what we're dealing with, people."

No one in the room had ever been in contact with a professional criminal like Everet. Before anyone could say anything, Emile said, "there's more, and it's more serious."

Everyone froze. Was Everet who he said he was, or were they looking at an imposter? After all, the guy was from Port Detour, not Detroit or Atlantic City or even Scarborough.

Emile took a moment to make sure he wanted to do this. The information from Spike was highly confidential. It couldn't be used to hurt people and he, Emile, certainly would tell no one where his information came from. He went ahead.

"Everet's current occupation is laundering money for organized crime. We think that's why he's moved back to Port Detour. Something's going on we don't know about."

No one moved a muscle. No one looked at the person next to them. They all stared at Emile.

"I know what you're thinking," continued Emile. "How could there be an organized crime guy in our community? Well, it happens, you know. They don't have their own exclusive town or area, organized crime is everywhere."

"No way," exclaimed Gail. "In Port Detour? Who else, Emile? My hairdresser is originally from New Jersey. His last name is Bertolli. Like the olive oil. Is he mafia?"

Emile didn't have time to answer, distracted by a question from Forest. "Are we in danger?"

"Not unless you insult him or look at him sideways," said Emile. The surrounding faces froze. He then added, "Just kidding."

Marg couldn't stand it any longer. She stood up, attracting everyone's attention.

"I've got something else," she announced. "It's to do with me."

Nobody said anything, still reeling from the knowledge of a convicted organized crime person in their circle of acquaintances. What now?

Marg spoke quickly, the pent-up thoughts of forty years rushing to be released.

"When I was nineteen, I went to a party and got blotto. My fault, for sure. But it wasn't my fault that I was then raped by two of the guys at the party. It's affected me my entire life and still does. Now's my chance to get rid of my demons."

Gail spoke up. "That's horrible, Marg. You must have been traumatized. Nobody could imagine what you've been through. But what do you mean? How are you going to get rid of your demons and why does it have anything to do with our wanting to find out more about the Overland brothers?"

As she spoke, a look of realization crossed her face and she raised her hand to her mouth. "Oh, my God. You mean the Overlands, don't you? They raped you. What a terrible thing, and you have had to deal with Kendrick for over two years, and now, Everet."

She got up from her chair, crossed over to Marg, and held her tight. Marg tried to protest, unsuccessfully. By now, the entire group crowded around Marg and for the first time in their association going back forty years, everyone saw Marg crying. Now everyone cried, men included.

Gail spoke first, voicing what was on everyone's mind. "Why are you telling us this, Marg? You didn't have to, you know."

Marg was now back to character, her voice firm and strong.

"That's easy, Gail. Those two are now going to pay for what they did. And it's going to hurt them even more that what they did to me." Now she was smiling, a contagious action that spread to the group.

"Ooh, what are you up to? It sounds diabolical. I love it," said Dakari.

"All in good time, folks. You're guaranteed to have front row seats."

Chapter 28

The results of the election were close. Rollie boasted it was a landslide. He won the mayorship and his three sidekicks were similarly elected councillors. Rollie and his buddies now controlled the Port Detour Council.

Rollie's election headquarter was a vacant storefront on Main Street. The previous business, Mainly Marijuana, the first marijuana outlet in the town, had gone bust. The owners realized too late that their fascination with marijuana didn't mean everyone in town felt the same way.

Rollie's Mayoral acceptance speech was delivered within ten minutes of the polls closing. His supporters crowded the space, the majority decidedly under forty years of age.

Rollie stood on the only chair in the store.

"Thanks for your support, folks. You believed in me and my running mates and now it's our turn to deliver what we promised. Our first council meeting will take place tomorrow evening. We'll be sworn in and then get down to work. You're going to see action, my friends, like you've never seen before. In two weeks, this town is going from a has-been to a beacon of light and opportunity. And we're going to get rid of the waste. Your taxes are going down."

Everybody raised their beer glasses and cheered.

Rollie stepped off the chair and motioned for the town clerk to come over.

"Ralph, I want to have a council meeting every day for the next week. Schedule it."

Ralph balked. "Mr. Mayor, that's impossible. The staff will have to work a lot of overtime to organize that."

Rollie looked at Ralph for a fleeting moment, locking eyes on the short, pudgy man.

"So? What's your point?"

"Nothing, sir. Is there anything else?"

"Yeah," replied Rollie. "Let's get some revenue for this town. Show the citizens we mean business. Have we got anything we can sell? Something the town doesn't need?"

Ralph was now intimidated and realized action was the new measure of success. "We got some old equipment we need to get rid of, sir."

"Naw, that's peanuts," said Rollie. "Something big. Something that'll make headlines."

"Let me think about it, sir." Ralph had been town clerk long enough to know what was being asked of him was also a test. It was best if he was a publicly devoted follower of his new boss. Without hesitation, he showed his support for Mayor Overland. "I'm sure I can find something. Maybe some excess land or buildings?"

"Now you're talking, Ralph. Why don't you look into that empty lot just north of the town hall? I believe the town owns it. In fact, it's been for sale for some time. The price is too high, though. Include that in your review."

"That's an excellent suggestion, Mayor Overland. I'll get right on it."

"Good boy, Ralph. I knew I could count on you."

Chapter 29

The next evening, at precisely six PM, Ralph rose from his seat at the side of the Council chambers. It was less than twenty-four hours after Rollie was elected mayor.

All seats in the council room were occupied. Rollie's rhetoric and promise of pursing justice for past councillors' misdeeds had resulted in a surge of interest from the ratepayers. The smell of beer permeated the room, the result of a start of six o'clock and more than a few pub dinners by the attendees.

"Call to order, ladies and gentlemen," Ralph announced. "It's time to invest our new mayor and councillors."

He walked to the centre of the chambers, motioned for Rollie to come forward and, with great ceremony and formal words, draped the chain of office over Rollie's shoulders and then swore the other councillors in. The attendees in the packed chambers clapped. Rollie bowed and said, "I now declare this council open for business. What's the first item on the agenda, Mr. Clerk?"

Ralph reached down to his desk, picked up, and opened a thick brown file. He extracted a paper-clipped group of sheets. "The first agenda item is an information announcement. This sheet," he held up one typewritten sheet, "is the plan which this Council intends to follow to raise revenues and cut expenses." He looked up at Rollie, who nodded his head to continue.

"It comprises five items, as follows. Sell land not required for immediate purposes, reduce the Works Department budget, eliminate the Parks and Recs department, reduce the number of police and also the number of firemen."

The crowd sitting in the gallery was momentarily silent. One person put up their hand, requesting to speak.

"Please introduce yourself, sir, and approach the mic," said Ralph. The flood waters had been released. Dozens of hands went up, as did the voice level.

"My name is Roy Maquire," said the gentleman at the mic. "If I understand what you said, you're going to reduce the budget of every department in the town. Now I don't enjoy paying taxes, but haven't you taken this too far? Who's going to replace the people let go, because that is the only way you can get costs down."

Mayor Overland rose to his feet. "Let's not get too worked up over this. Sure, we're going to let people go, but that's what you elected me for. Our taxes are too high. Everyone of you have told me. I'm just taking the action you asked for." He sat down.

Another gentleman approached the mic. "Yeah, but we didn't tell you we wanted to cut back on the services. If my house is on fire, who's going to put it out? This is short-sighted, young man."

Rollie rose again. "We have a plan. Your services won't be cut. Let's talk about something that doesn't affect anyone here and could put millions in the town's bank account." He paused, looked at a few faces, and waited until the sound level reduced.

"Do you know the town has millions of dollars tied up in real estate we'll never use? The town clerk and I had an excellent discussion yesterday about this very thing. Ralph, why don't you explain what we found?"

Ralphs extracted a stapled group of pages from his briefcase and slowly rose, turning to face the audience. He looked at the first page and then waved it at the crowd.

"The vacant lot just north of the town hall is a good example. It was bought from some councillors years ago and we never found a use for it. In fact, nobody knows why the town bought it in the first place."

Rollie interjected, "How's that for graft, folks? Keep going Ralph."

Ralph continued. "This is a good example of how we can raise revenues. The town doesn't need it and we should sell it. It's zoned commercial, so if it were properly priced, I'm sure it could be sold within a year."

Rollie again interrupted Ralph. "Anybody object to that?" The crowd was silent.

"Good," continued Rollie. "Before the election, I did some research and not only identified the excess land, but I lined up buyers who will pay cash for that specific lot. Prior to this, nobody has shown any interest in it. If we sell, the money we receive will reduce your taxes."

"How much?" somebody yelled.

Rollie was ready. "By at least ten percent," he flippantly said, tossing out an appealing number to the taxpayers. The crowd was now silent. "But let's leave the budget cuts for now until we have more information. I think you will agree, though. We can certainly go ahead with land sales."

The three new councillors, Rollie's handpicked candidates, jumped to their feet and clapped. The two returning councillors sat with blank faces, no agreement or objection evident.

Rollie continued. "I think I can have the details tomorrow night. We've got council meetings scheduled for every night, so we'll tackle this costs thing first. It's the beginning of a new era, folks. Trust me."

Gail turned to Marg. The Blue Duck people were all present, sitting beside each other in the third row on recycled church benches. Marg thought the words 'trust me' probably offended The Almighty, but as usual, he was silent. Gail whispered, "Sounds too good to be true, Marg." Marg turned to her. "Exactly what I was thinking, Gail."

An audience member approached the mic and asked, "When is this sale supposed to take place, Mayor?"

Rollie had a ready answer. "This week. Maybe tomorrow or the next day. I said I found a buyer. We have received no other realistic offers, other than one for one million." Rollie wasn't forthcoming about who had made the low-ball bid and no one asked.

The meeting went on for another three hours. Few details were offered about how the cost cutting would be handled and the impact on services. The Blue Duck members stood in a group after the meeting had been adjourned.

"This land sale sounds too good to be true," said Rey Rey.

"That's what I already said, Rey Rey. Who bought it?" asked Gail.

Marg offered her opinion. "You're right. It's too good to be true. Indeed, who bought it? Forest, you're the detail man. Can you keep track of this land deal?"

This was right up Forest's alley. He had been concerned with detail all his life.

"Find out exactly what's happening. Who's the buyer? What price did the town agree to? Confirm that the money is paid, OK?"

"I already know one thing, Marg. The land is listed for five million. No wonder it didn't sell."

Before they broke up, Dakari asked, "When should we meet again? I don't really know what's going on."

Marg assumed command and spoke with confidence. "Let's wait until the property sale goes through and the town has its money. You'll have more information by then, Forest. We can then have a meeting to explore this in more detail."

No one objected. "Where, Marg?" asked Gail.

"Dakari's place is great. OK Dakari?"

He nodded and Marg added, "I'll call everyone when I know the sale has gone through. I'm also working on some related details. We can cover those at the same time."

'Related details' raced through everyone's head. This was more exciting than waiting to find out the winner of the Agricultural Fair best pie contest.

Chapter 30

The sound of a bugle blasted from the brightly polished bar of the Blue Duck Tavern. Kendrick put down the towel and the glass, picked up his cell phone, and pressed the answer icon.

"Well, is it set up?" asked Everet, with no greeting. His voice sounded nervous. Most unusual for his brother, he thought.

"Yep, everything was set up first thing this morning. The numbered company is now official and Marg has arranged the banking. We're all set."

Everet continued, his usual arrogant and loud voice back on display.

"Great. I'm arranging for some money to be transferred. What name did you use?"

"It's a number, Everet, not a name. It's 418064 Ontario Limited."

For a minute, there was silence. "Are you still there, Everet?"

"What about Marg? She set all this up, right? Can we trust her? "

Everet was never one to care about details, and yet here he was, questioning Marg's trustworthiness for the third time. A con man worried about trust—ironic, Kendrick thought.

"She was a partner in one of the most prestigious law firms in Toronto. Also, do you recall her telling us that numbered companies are not required to disclose their ownership? You client is into security and I imagine privacy is a valued commodity."

"You're right. No one can know who is behind this company. What about Marg? You got her to set it up, right? Can we trust her?"

He didn't seem to realize he had asked the same question one minute ago.

"And you're sure she did this properly and legally?"

"I'd trust her with anything, Everet. I'm sure she knows how to form a company."

"I'm detecting something here, bro. Why wouldn't she know how to do this with her eyes closed?"

"Well, you know she was a criminal lawyer, not a corporate lawyer?"

There was complete silence on the other end of the phone. The only thing Kendrick heard was the swishing of the ceiling fans and the clink of the dishwasher.

"Are you there, Everet?"

"Yeah, I'm here. I gotta go. I'll call when the money is sent. Goodbye."

Three phone calls were made between three and four o'clock.

Everet called Kendrick. "The money has been sent. It's five million dollars. I'll call you later with more info, but it looks like we're going to buy some excess land from the town. It'll be a brilliant spot for the new building. I just need approval from my clients."

At three-thirty, Kendrick's phone rang. It was Everet. "Have the bank prepare a bank draft for two million dollars made out to the Town of Port Detour and send it over to the town clerk."

The last call was from Freddy to Marg, the designated signing officer, asking that she come into the bank and sign the paper and the draft.

Marg took the draft with her and made the short trip to city hall. She handed the envelope containing the draft to the town clerk and asked for a receipt. She paused briefly in the entranceway and made four phone calls, each with the same message.

"It's done. Let's get together at Dakari's house at seven in the evening, the day after tomorrow. All the papers and the money should be processed by then. See you there."

Chapter 31

The Council meeting next evening was jam-packed. People stood in the hallway, hoping to hear even one small smidgeon of conversation. For those who couldn't hear, the words were relayed from the people seated in the council chambers. Mayor Overland opened the meeting promptly on time. Before they could get to agenda item number one, the sale of land, one of the audience members jumped up and commandeered the mic.

"Who are you planning to lay off, Rollie? We need answers."

The council chamber erupted into chaos. Voices clashed, and the volume level rose like a tidal wave to a deafening level.

Rollie yelled out, "Order, order" a dozen times, and the turmoil died down only when he jumped up on his desk, wildly waving his arms and motioning for the lone policeman monitoring the meeting to come to the front. The sight of a uniform had the desired effect. The large woman in the front row stopped shaking her fist and sat down, the near silence providing an opening for Ralph. In an impassive voice, he introduced agenda item number one - the sale of a town-owned lot at the corner of Freeland and Main streets–and sat down.

Rollie slowly rose to take the mic. He looked around cautiously, apparently expecting some comment. "I'd like to call on our solicitor, Morley Wanting, to explain this sale."

"Not much to explain, Mr. Mayor. This is a great deal. We have it on our books at a value of five million dollars, but this is somebody's hallucination. It's not worth anywhere near that amount. More like a million. The town should take advantage of this before it's withdrawn."

The discussion was brief. Rollie promised a tax reduction, an offer that no one could object to. Now the audience couldn't hold back their enthusiasm for the deal.

The councillors unanimously passed the motion to sell. The large lady in the front row now shouted out, "Great job, Mr. Mayor. Well done." Rollie smiled from ear to ear, completely ignoring the fickleness of his supporter.

Talk of future staff layoffs disappeared in the excitement of having sold what everyone knew to be a worthless asset. Rollie continued to extoll the deal, making his words sound as if he were the best negotiator in the country. The rest of the meeting touched on the downsizing of various departments, but details were few. Rollie successfully provided just enough information to quell the revolt and defer the items until tomorrow's meeting.

The thoughts rolling around Rollies' mind were positive. Tomorrow was another day. People forget quickly and anyway, he, the Mayor, was going to reduce taxes for everyone. How could anyone argue against that?

Another person was ecstatic. Everet Overland attended the meeting, standing on the periphery. He immediately made a cell phone call.

"It's done. You now own the property. Congrats."

Next evening's meeting was a repeat of the previous night's. Again, the council chambers were packed, and the overflow extended well down the hallway. But there was one difference. The euphoria of last night had disappeared. Instead of smiles, one could see frowns and hear muttering. Most people were standing, talking angrily to the person next to them.

"Agenda item number one is the downsizing of the Parks and Recreation department." intoned Ralph.

There was a mad rush to the microphones. The comments took Rollie aback. It was apparent downsizing was not popular, given the comments, especially from the mothers. Rollie proposed that the budget be reduced by fifty per cent and keep a reduced department.

The vote was close, but it resulted in a fifty percent reduction in expenses. The department was saved, not eliminated. Not too bad, thought Rollie. This was a sacred cow. Maybe it would work for the other departments.

The proposed reductions in budget for the police and the fire departments proved him wrong. The comments from the gallery were consistent and negative. Reduce the budgets at your peril, was the message.

Rollie appealed. "But the cuts will reduce your taxes, folks. Why can't you see that?"

The first speaker after that comment was blunt. "We can't see it, Mr. Stupid, because crime is up and so are fire calls. Get real. Where have you been?"

That hurt. The continuing discussion proved more caustic and more personal. He remembered being made fun of in grade 7. Rollie shut the meeting down ten minutes later. The local newspaper reported that the mayor claimed it wasn't because somebody threatened to shoot him,

"Nobody can intimidate Rollie Overland," he was reported to say. The picture accompanying the article showed a head shot of a person with wild eyes and his hair arranged as if hit by a hurricane.

Rollie, after the meeting, got stuck amid the crowd exiting the building and easily heard Lynda Garrison's loud comment to her sister. "Fred's going to be really pissed off if this happens. He's been in the fire department for years. Wait until the next fire. I'll be damned if I'm going to let my house burn down because of missing staff. This guy's an idiot. He should be lynched."

The thought of fleeing crossed Rollie's mind. He was too young to die.

Chapter 32

Two days later, at seven o'clock, the Blue Duck members arrived en masse at Dakari's house. Everyone realized their efforts to find out what the Overland brothers had done for the past forty years made for a fascinating story. Maybe even movie material.

Rey Rey brought up the possibility as they were waiting to start the meeting.

"I think Robert Redford could play Kendrick. I'm have a hard time deciding who should play me. Robert DeNiro, do you think?" It was contagious. Now everyone voiced their thoughts, not realizing they had stepped out of reality.

"Get real, everyone," said Marg. "The story isn't finished yet. Remember, I said I knew of some 'related details'. I can now tell you that something has been put in place that will make Rollie's election and the family gang he is part of wish they hadn't tangled with Marg O'Toole."

She smiled and looked around the group, totally relaxed. Even her clothes choice today was relaxed. White runners, bell bottom, loose linen pants and a big turtleneck sweater. Unusual for Marg, her hair tumbled down loosely with a single barret holding it back from her face. Nobody in the room could deny she was in control.

"OK, let's get to the juicy part. I don't mind admitting that nothing would give me more pleasure than seeing the Overlands taken down. I think the wheels are in motion right now to make that happen."

"What do you mean, 'taken down' Marg?" asked Gail.

"Whatever you think it is, Gail. The only limit is your imagination."

"I like that," said Dakari. "I vote for death. I can see the painting right now. Kind of like Guernica by Picasso. I'll make it big, a masterpiece."

"I'd hate to be inside your head, Dakari. How do you come up with these crazy ideas?"

Dakari beamed. Marg continued on with her plan. "Kendrick asked me to." Her cell phone rang.

She glanced at the caller ID and said to the group, "Speak of the devil. It looks like you need to get in your front row seats right now. The show is about to start." She put her fingers up to her lips, made a shush sound and then pressed the speaker icon.

"Hi Kendrick. What's new?" she said sweetly. Everyone looked at each other, quietly laughing, until Marg put up her hand to signify quiet.

Kendrick's voice was louder than usual. Everyone could hear everything, even without the speaker. "Marg, we've got a big problem. We need to see you. As soon as possible, Marg." His voice wavered, the swagger completely absent.

"Who's we, Kendrick? You and Everet? What do you need to see me about?"

"We have to talk to you and find out what's happened, Marg. This is a big screw-up, an enormous screw-up. Where are you? We need to meet right away."

"No can do, Kendrick. I'm busy right now. How about sometime next week?"

"Next week? No way, Marg. This must happen right now. Don't you understand? You might have done something wrong."

"I never do anything wrong, Kendrick. What are you talking about?"

Marg turned to the group, an enormous smile on her face. She's enjoying this, thought Gail.

"The numbered company, Marg. And the bank account. Something's terribly wrong. We have to get this fixed up right now. Everet's investors are really pissed off. We'll lose them if we can't fix this."

"OK, OK, if it's that important. I'm with Dakari at his studio. You know where that is. Why don't you come up now? I'm here for another thirty minutes."

"Don't leave, Marg. We'll be there ASAP."

Everyone heard the knock on Dakari's front door. Marg's mouth went dry, knowing what was going to happen. Not that it bothered her. She had experienced a situation like this many times in her career. It was the rush of adrenaline and it always happened right before her clients were accused of committing a crime.

Dakari walked from the studio to answer the knock, opened the front door and was almost bowled over by the two brothers rush to enter. As usual, Everet was dressed to impress, while Kendrick looked like he just got out of bed, wearing torn jeans and a T-shirt, no socks. But it was their heads that communicated their states of mind. There was a wildness in their eyes and their dishevelled hair evidenced panic. Dakari could smell the fear.

"Where is she, Dakari?" demanded Everet.

"If you're referring to Marg, she's back in the studio with the others."

"Others? What others?" asked Everet.

"The Blue Duck people. They've been making enquiries about you two, didn't you know? C'mon, let's hear what they want to discuss with you."

This new bit of information had a dampening effect on the brothers' urgency. They looked at each other with concern, slowed their pace and followed Dakari down the hall to his studio at the rear of the house.

Everet slowed the pace even more. Kendrick almost bumped into him.

He whispered to Kendrick. "Slow down, Kendrick. I need time to think. Something's wrong."

"Nice digs, Dakari," said Everet. He made a pretence of examining some of Dakari's art pieces hanging on the walls. They all were dark and gloomy, created when Dakari was going through his artistic "dark" period. The word 'premonition' popped into his mind.

"Looks like a wonderful space to develop some evil ideas," said Everet. If they only knew, thought Dakari.

The door to the studio was open and the other five Blue Duck members came into view, seated randomly around the room. Marg O'Toole, with no greeting, got up from her chair and motioned for them to take seats next to each other.

"We'll stand, Marg," said Everet. "What you screwed up shouldn't take long to correct."

"Well, since I really don't know what you think I screwed up, it might take a lot longer than you expect. Anyway, do you know what I'm accusing you of? Both of you?"

Kendrick frowned. What was she talking about? As far as he knew, Everet was only concerned with the money, that's all.

"That's a laugh," said Everet. "I'm the one doing the accusing, not you." He scowled at Marg. "Let's get on with it. You've got some correcting to do."

He spoke as if she was some lower person who had crossed a superior being's path. I can't believe that, thought Gail. She saw wild hair and one undone button on his shirt. Kendrick had retreated behind Everet, eyes downcast.

Marg said nothing and moved to the centre of the room. She stood within spitting distance of Everet without looking at him.

"Here's the correction, you two. Right now, you don't acknowledge it, but before we're finished, you will." She slowly unfolded her left arm to point to the display board covered with coloured notes and handwritten comments from their last meeting.

"You're looking at an interesting tale, gentlemen, and it's all about you. It requires some explanation to fully understand it, since it's a two-part explanation, but it won't take long since you already know the story."

Kendrick and Everet's faces took on an exasperated look. Then, as if somebody pulled a puppet string, they both raised their arms, their palms facing out.

"More bullshit. Enough with the games, Marg," said Everet. "What's this all about? Kendrick and I could lose millions because of your incompetence. Our reputations are at stake here."

"Oh, Everet, it's more than your reputations at stake. It's your lives."

Her nervousness disappeared. It always did when she was in court. She slowly turned around, catching everyone's eye, not saying anything. Finally, her eyes rested on Kendrick and Everet.

"Everet, you're a fucking liar, and Kendrick, you're a coward. You say you don't remember me or an incident forty years ago. That is bullshit with a capital B. Do you remember a high school party, Everet? Do you remember raping me, while you," she pointed to Kendrick, "held me down?"

The studio's north-facing windows allowed the full sun to come in and whether it was deliberate, her position in the room caused her body to be lit up as if she were under a spotlight. There was not one sound in the room. Nobody in the room knew what to do. They stared at Marg, then at Everet, then at Kendrick. They looked at each other, everyone with the same thought. Was it true? Why was Marg saying all this?

Everet's face, during Marg's harangue, took on the look of a bored listener. He crossed his legs and examined his fingernails at length. When Marg finished, he looked around the group.

"Never happened, Marg, never happened. You sound like a crazed fool. You're hallucinating. Is this why you had to retire from your firm? Did you partners see something you won't admit to? Anyway, if you really believe that, why didn't you do something about it? What proof do you have?"

"I've got proof, Everet. But let's hear from Kendrick. He was there as well."

All eyes shifted to Kendrick, who lowered his head, slumped his shoulders, stared off into space and was silent. Marg was annoyed.

"Kendrick, are you here? Talk to us."

Kendrick's voice was so low, everyone had to strain to hear it. "It's partly true. Marg is partly right about the rape, but it never happened."

Marg's stance became rigid. Why was Kendrick saying this?

"What do you mean, Kendrick? It never happened?"

"You were pretty sloshed that night. In fact, Everet had to help you upstairs in the big house to the bedroom. Anyway, I became concerned when I didn't see Everet come back and I went upstairs to see what happened. I couldn't believe what I saw."

He continued, not looking at anyone.

"I found Everet on the bed on top of you. He had removed nearly all your clothes, and I assumed you had been raped. I grabbed his arms and pulled him off you, but I don't think you knew what was happening. Everet was really pissed off, swore and tried to fight with me. I guess I was more sober than he was because I got him out of the room and saw him go downstairs. When he left, I dressed you as best I could."

"That's bullshit, Kendrick. Everet raped me, you know that. Are you trying to tell me and this group that you're a good Samaritan?"

"Yeah, Marg. That's what I am. Do you really want to know why?"

He didn't wait for an answer.

"I'm the one who brought you to the hospital. If you want proof of that, just ask to see the hospital admittance records and see who signed you in. It was me, Marg, me."

"I know that, Kendrick. I already have a copy of the records."

"You already have a copy? Did you read it, Marg, did you?" he said in a voice close to shouting. He had brought both arms up, his fists were clenched and his face was distorted with rage.

"So, Marg, it's your time to tell the truth. Were you raped or not? What did the results of your examination show? Care to tell us?"

"I don't know, Kendrick. I've had them for years but never looked at them. Who wants to relive a nightmare? Anyway, I already know what's in them."

"Do you, Marg? Really?" said Kendrick. Everet stood near his brother, a nasty-looking grin plastered on his face.

Marg opened her bag and pulled a manila envelope out, extracted the papers inside and read them. It only took a minute, and she then put them back in the envelope and her bag. Her hands shook, and she thought how stupid she was. Why hadn't she read this years ago? Emile moved from his chair and picked up her hand, giving it a squeeze. She was near tears.

"Well, Marg. Were you raped or not?" asked Kendrick. "And who brought you to the hospital?"

"You're right. I wasn't raped, Kendrick. For forty years I thought I had, that I was damaged goods. Apparently I was wrong. And you're listed as the person who brought me in."

Everet was quick with a comment. "Who's lying now, Marg?" He turned to face the spectators. "It looks like our big shot lawyer just got hoisted on her own petard. I'm sure you understand what that means? Where's the apology, Marg? While you're at it, where's the money you owe us? "

Slowly, she raised her head. Her body stood erect, her head slowly rotated as her eyes directly looked at each person. With a steely voice, she said, "I won't apologize for what you intended to do, Everet. If Kendrick hadn't shown up, I would have been raped by you."

She then moved forward to face Kendrick. "Thank you, Kendrick, sincerely. What you did for me was a lifesaver." Her mind was working overtime now. "I'm sorry, Kendrick. I now realize it was all Everet, wasn't it?"

"Yes it was, Marg."

Marg stood still, looking intently at Kendrick. Her lips quivered and everyone in the group could see she was hesitating, that she had something else to say.

"Kendrick, I have a confession. I know another reason you left Port Detour. I know you think you murdered a young man named Bart Brown. I read the police reports. You had a fight with him at a tavern and I guess you thought you killed him. Am I right?"

Kendrick nodded his head vigorously, a few tears appearing in his eyes. "Yeah, I killed him. I panicked and fled."

"You're wrong, Kendrick. You gave him a concussion, that's it. But it no doubt looked like he was dead. There must have been an awful lot of blood on the ground. He's alive and well, Kendrick."

Kendrick was frozen. Forty years of guilt wiped away.

Emile wasn't that sentimental or distracted so easily. Whether or not Kendrick was guilty made no difference to him. He was now focussed on Everet. He ignored the scene playing out in front of him, dropped Marg's hand and stepped in front of her.

"Just to be clear, what Everet did is assault, plain and simple. What's even worse is the fact he intended to rape her while she was unconscious, unable to protect herself. And a male against a female? No contest. People like Everet are nothing but monsters, taking advantage of a situation. I'll take it upon myself to bring charges, Everet."

Everet's grin disappeared, and he sat down on the nearest chair.

Emile held both her hands now. She looked directly at Everet. "You're an asshole, Everet. And you're also a criminal."

Suddenly, her demeanour changed, and she walked around the room at a slow, deliberate pace. Her voice grew firmer, her words were carefully spaced.

"We aren't finished with you, Everet. Did I not hear, when you came in, that you accused me of screwing up something?"

"You're hearing is perfect, lady. It's too bad your abilities aren't the same." He turned around in his chair and faced the others. "Big talk from a fraud. You heard her. She accused me of raping her when I did no such thing. She's even brought the proof for us to see. I can hardly wait to hear how she screwed up my deal with new investors for our town."

He turned back to Marg. "Go ahead. Since you've already made a false accusation about me, who's going to believe what you have to say now?"

Chapter 33

Marg started pacing, as if in a courtroom, looked down at the floor periodically and then into the faces of Rey Rey, Dakari, Gail, Forest and Emile. She never stopped smiling.

Slowly she came to a stop in front of Everet, looked down at him and said, "Let's make sure I understood what you asked me to do."

Everet shrugged. "If you want Marg. But whatever you did, didn't work. You're incompetent."

Marg continued. "You let Kendrick carry your message to me. You wanted a private company formed with the ownership hidden if anyone came searching. Right?"

"Yeah, pretty simple, huh?"

"Then you needed the bank account set up the same day so you could deposit a big pile of money and buy some spare land from the town. I even had the bank send the town a cheque for two mill, Right?"

He nodded.

"So, what's the problem? What did I screw up?"

"You know what you did, lady. And it was deliberate. My client sent the bank five mill, we used two mill, and he wants to other three mill back. Now I find I can't do it."

As he finished the sentence, beads of sweat broke out on his brow. He took the white handkerchief from his breast pocket, wiped off the sweat, and crumpled the handkerchief into a ball in his hand.

"Why not?" she asked in a pleasant, enquiring tone.

Everet jumped from his chair, took three paces to reach Marg, and put his finger within inches of her face.

"Because you screwed me, you bitch. The bank won't talk to me. The bank doesn't even know my name. They won't even acknowledge my signing authority. They've never seen my signature." His face was contorted with rage.

Marg slowly pushed his finger away with her index finger. She calmly asked, "And why do you think that is?"

Everet shrugged.

She continued. "I thought you didn't want your name associated with the company. Kendrick didn't say you wanted to have signing authority. I assumed you left that up to me."

"Well, you're wrong, you dumb broad." He looked over at his brother. "And Kendrick is just as stupid as you are. Fix it, right now."

"Not unless you apologize for those bad words you said about me."

Everet frowned. Everyone stared at him, wondering if he could do that. A minute ticked by.

"I apologize. Now fix it."

"Naw, I don't think so, Everet. You don't really mean it and anyway, you haven't apologized for raping me."

"God damn it, I didn't rape you."

Marg faced him with no expression on her face.

"Didn't you hear me? I did nothing wrong."

Marg hadn't moved an inch, nor did she say anything.

Everet now mouthed the conclusion that had formed in his mind. "You're going to screw me, aren't you, Miss High and Mighty?"

Forest had now figured it out. Everet and his client would never get their money back.

Everet was now shouting. "I'll sue. My client will sue. Then we'll see who has to apologize."

"That's bullshit, Everet. We know you're laundering mob money from Syracuse and New York. No one is going to sue. In fact, no one can find out who owns the company. That was your request, wasn't it?"

She took a step forward, making Everet back up.

"No Everet, if I were you, I'd run. I'd run fast and far. Right now, your life isn't worth as much as those fancy loafers you have on."

The entire group could feel the tension rise even higher. Now what?

"I'm not running, Marg. I want signing authority. My client wants his money back and I'll be damned if a two-bit female lawyer is going to stop me. I have no intention of being a hunted man."

"Do you mean hunted, like in extinction, Everet? I'll take odds on that one. I don't see what I can do to help you, Everet. Good luck."

"Good luck to you, too," he shouted. "My clients will quickly find out who has their money. It'll be you they are after, not me."

Everet's arms were rigid against his sides and his hands were tightly curled into fists. Everyone waited for the blows to come. Marg held her ground. Everet almost spat in Marg's face.

"Last chance, lady. Give me what is rightly mine."

Marg slowly shook her head, her facial expression blank and her eyes unblinking.

"Your funeral, big shot." Everet spun on his heel and walked to the front door. He grabbed it so forcefully the door swung rapidly back and the sound of it hitting the wall reverberated throughout the house. Two paintings on the wall fell to the floor. With one backward glare, Everet disappeared.

The sound of the door hitting the wall jolted Marg's logic. Until now, she ignored the fact that Everet represented the mob. The money she now had control over wasn't hers, and the owners were not nice people. Violent people, if she was honest. Had she jumped out of the pot into the fire? She couldn't make it go away right now and she was in a room with her best friends, everyone of them looking directly at her.

Especially Forest, who looked frightened, not even aware of Marg's precarious position. He had seen no one's face look as hard as Marg's and as angry as Everet's. He was frozen and ever so slightly moved his eyes to see the reaction from the other people in the room. By the horrified looks on everyone's faces, they seemed to experience the same thing. Had Marg just given Everet the death penalty? Or had she given herself one?

Rey Rey whispered to Forest on his left. "Do you think we're on the hit list along with Everet and Marg? We're all members of the same club."

"I dunno, Rey Rey. Could be." He spoke directly to Marg. "Are we in any danger, Marg?"

"You're OK, Rey Rey and so is everyone else. But that's my opinion, and my suggestion is you don't breathe a word of this to anyone. Some people may not think so kindly about what you now know. If anyone asks, you've heard nothing. Deny everything if you value your life." A slight smile crossed her face.

Forest, Gail, and Rey Rey swiftly stampeded out the front door.

Emile got up from his chair and sidled over to Marg. "That was a little thick, don't you think?"

"Emile, I think most people live rather humdrum lives. Something like this is what you talk about for all your remaining days. It's the excitement that keeps us going, Emile. You don't get that shopping for groceries. I just gave them a gift."

Kendrick had hung back, avoiding the stampede, and overheard Marg's comment to Emile.

"Marg, not everybody thinks the way you do. This affair with Everet is more than I ever wanted. Even with my casual involvement, I could be on a hit list, couldn't I?"

"Don't flatter yourself, Kendrick. Everet's connections probably don't know you exist." His face went slack, and he had a pained look.

Marg looked around and spoke to the remaining attendees. "I think we're done here, guys. Emile, I know it's late but how about I prepare my pasta dish, the one you said was to die for? You bring the wine and I'll bring my culinary skills and my scintillating personality."

"You're on Marg," said the lawman, his eyes now glowing with anticipation.

Kendrick stood still, like a silent appendage. Marg looked at him, conflicting thoughts running through her head. Kendrick wasn't as bad as she thought for the last forty years.

"Hey Kendrick, why don't you join us? I've got an idea that is more suited to your good nature."

Kendrick, above all, wanted to be liked. His bravado made up for a lot of insecurity. But an invitation from Marg?

"Let me check my calendar, Marg." He pretended to look at his cell phone. "Just the Prime Minister. Yeah, I can make it. He can wait." His laughter filled the studio.

She turned to Dakari. "Of course you're going to come, Dakari. Right?"

"Wouldn't miss it for the world, Marg. Probably give us a chance to hear about your plans for the three million."

Marg, in a low voice, replied, "I guess."

Never without words, Dakari asked, "What? Aren't you going to let us know? You apparently have full control of it now. I'd also like to know how long Everet, and maybe Rollie, have."

"Have?" asked Kendrick.

"You know," said Dakari. "When will they be bumped off if he can't get the money back to the mob?"

"That's pure speculation, Dakari," said Emile. "I think both Marg and Everet were a little over-dramatic. People say the most terrible things when they are stressed or under pressure. Just dial it back a little in your brains. Nothing that violent is going to happen."

Marg agreed. "Hey, why don't I invite Rey Rey, Gail and Forest also? We'll make it a party."

Driving home, Marg couldn't dismiss Everet's comment. As long as she had the money, she was on a hit list. Easily solved, she thought. Just give it back. Another thought popped into her mind. Why not?

Chapter 34

The four of them left Dakari's house, moving as a group down the front walk. The sun had set, leaving a ghostly glow on the surrounding terrain. Emile and Marg were at the rear, everyone trying to see the walk, which was now in deep shadow.

A gunshot rang out and everyone heard the bullet hit the door frame behind them. Emile immediately moved to the front of the group and pushed each one down on the brown lawn bordering the walkway. He then crouched low and moved to the street, looking around both ways. Nothing.

"Everyone OK?" he yelled back. Kendrick, Dakari and Marg were back on the walk, everyone upright and no evidence of a wound.

"We're fine, Emile," yelled Marg. "What just happened? Did somebody just shoot at us?"

Emile had returned to the group and stood facing them.

"Oh, one of us was the target, all right. And it came from a passing car, the only one nearby. Didn't you hear a car speed up after the shot?"

"Sorry, that wasn't top of my mind, Emile," said Kendrick. "I know a gunshot when I hear it, and I also know that bullets can kill you. All I wanted to do was stay low and flat. Thanks for the quick thinking." The other two nodded in agreement.

Marg had regained her composure and her instincts kicked in. "Emile, do you think whoever fired at us wanted to kill one of us?"

"No way, Marg. Remember the car that tried to run us down? That was meant to kill either you or I or both of us. Not this one. Whoever fired the shot deliberately missed us. They could easily have hit any of us, they were that close. No, this is something else."

Dakari hadn't fully recovered. He believed in and practised a life as a non-violent person. His voice quivered when he spoke.

"What do you mean, Emile? What's this 'something else'?"

"It's a warning, Dakari, and it's directed towards Marg, no one else."

As the realization of what he was saying sunk in, Marg wanted action. "Emile, tell your police friends to arrest Everet. He did this, right?"

"You're probably right, Marg. I'll call them, but where's the proof? Nobody saw him. The street was empty, not a single person on it, not even a guy walking his dog. He was in a car, so I'll bet there's no spent bullet casing on the ground."

The four of them stood in a group, not knowing what to do. Emil spoke first.

"We can't do anything here, so let's go to Marg's party. Marg, I'll go with you, if you don't mind."

Marg didn't mind in the least. Who could object to a handsome older man wanting to protect her?

They left Marg's car at Dakari's and Emile would drive her to the grocery store and then home. Both of them were silent on the brief trip, each lost in their own thoughts. Marg tried to overcome her fear of being a target and Emile smiled at the thought of being a protector. He dropped Marg off at her condo.

"I'll see you in a while, Marg."

Marg took the elevator and carried her groceries into the condo. She laid down her cell phone on the kitchen counter and noticed it was flashing. A message notification. Strange, she thought. I didn't hear a notice, but sometimes text messages didn't alert the user.

The message was brief. "Next time it's your legs."

The message didn't bother her as much as she imagined it would. She had a protector and an enjoyable evening to look forward to. She debated about whom to tell about the message. Only Emile, she decided.

Chapter 35

Marg felt good. The feeling one gets when you get together with friends. One friend in particular.

The meal prep was complete and the smell of tomato pasta sauce and garlic bread permeated the condo. The dining room table was set for eight and the bouquet of fresh flowers she bought on the way home provided a splash of colour and scent to the entire room.

Her thoughts turned to Emile. She had never felt this way about a man. Her entire life had been one of confrontation with them. She even had to convince the car salesman that it was she deciding, not her non-existent husband.

Emile was different, and so was she. Age can be kind if handled properly. It provides a different, more tolerant view of the world. You gradually learn, she thought, that people aren't perfect, least of all yourself. But there is no room for bitterness if you are the author of your own misfortune. She had chosen her lifestyle, and it never included a companion. Perhaps it was time to rethink that direction.

She heard the buzzer from the lobby, pushed the view button, and saw seven people right on time. "Come on up, fourth floor," she said, and within minutes welcomed her guests. Her condo was large by any standard, and the furnishings and decor were perfection personified, not marred by children or pets or a husband.

"Emile, can you handle the drink orders?" she asked.

"I'd love to, Marg," he responded. That was so easy, she thought. I could get used to this.

The evening was a roaring success. The guest combination worked to perfection. Kendrick dropped his smart ass pretence, Emile was a superb storyteller and Dakari was, well, Dakari. He knew everything there was to know, always presented from a wry perspective. The other three couldn't get a word in edge wise.

"Why don't we have our dessert and coffee and whatever you're drinking in the living room?" asked Marg. It was a popular suggestion, and they all sat around the conversation pit, completely relaxed. Marg not so much.

"So, Marg," asked Dakari, "what about the three million and the property you now control? You owe us an explanation about your little windfall. Or should I call it a confiscation?"

His pure white teeth glowed with the smile. His curly white hair stuck up everywhere, his mufti carelessly thrown on the rug like a captured rainbow.

Drink in hand, Marg leaned back and took a sip of her Grand Marnier.

"It's all mine, you know, but I also feel that it's owned by the Blue Duck Club. That's the only reason I have it. If the Blue Duck Social Club hadn't been here, then the money also wouldn't be here. It would still be in the US. It's ironic that Everet, the bad guy, is responsible for what you call a windfall."

"Marg, you're sure nobody can find out about the money? Where it is and who controls it?"asked Emile.

"The mob has all kinds of ways to find out info. They can bribe officials, they can force it out of Everet, but he doesn't really know that much. Anyway, the amount is small for the mob. I'm not sure how far they would go, but it would certainly publicize, and maybe jeopardize, their existence. No, I think we're safe."

In her mind, she knew that wasn't true. Forty years working in that world had taught her one thing above all. The mob doesn't forget. She would think of something when it happened. Right now, there was no need to alarm her cohorts. It would happen when it happened.

Dakari pursued his original question. "What are you going to do with it, Marg?"

"Personally, I'm not going to do anything with it, Dakari. We all are. What do you think of this idea?"

Marg looked at them for a good two minutes until her audience was uncomfortable and fidgeting. All they wanted now was something to agree to.

"The money will be the first contribution to the Blue Duck Charitable Trust." She paused and looked for a reaction.

"What's a charitable trust, Marg?" asked Dakari.

Forest cleared his throat and volunteered an explanation.

"We're going to support charitable activities, Dakari. It's a great idea. What do you think we should support, Marg?"

Marg now had their undivided attention.

"I have one in mind right now. I'm sure we can come up with more. The one I'm thinking of is in Port Detour. It's called Evergreen Gardens, and it needs financial support, otherwise it's going to have to declare bankruptcy. It's a care facility for handicapped people."

Dakari added, "I know it. It's on Peter Street, near the rec centre. I also know what they do. They provide a service that is sorely in need in our society. They support the forgotten people. Why haven't they got enough money, Marg? Surely the guardians of the residents have to pay for anybody they have in the home."

"It's not enough, Dakari. As it now stands, the guardians of the residents pay a lot of money, even to the point of depriving them of their own needs. But you know what's ironic?"

Everybody shook their head.

"When the facility was founded, it bought land which has turned out to be worth a lot of money today. But they also borrowed millions to finance it. They really need to pay off the debt and then they can operate soundly. No one has stepped forward so far. Next month, they'll have to declare bankruptcy, and all the residents will have to be moved to another facility."

She then explained how the trust would work, which facilities it could support, and how to choose which guardians and their dependents should be supported.

"So we have two problems. Some people don't have the income or resources to pay to support their loved ones? And second, what can be done to pay off their debt?"

She ended her explanation with a proposal.

"We can solve the debt repayment problem if we can find someone to pay off the debt. Then, with the three million that's controlled by the Blue Duck Charitable Trust, we can put the financial assistance plan in place. I know one individual who is hurting financially but would never admit it. He has a severely disabled daughter. I would like to nominate him to be the recipient of our first grant."

"Who's that Marg? Do we know this person?"

"You sure do. He's sitting in this room."

Rey Rey had been quiet and took the opportunity to make his presence known. "I get it, Marg. It's brilliant. We all know about Sandra." He looked at Kendrick. "You're very proud of your daughter, Kendrick. You've done a great job supporting her. What do you say? Do you need the support?"

Kendrick frowned and looked at everyone, an astonished look on his face.

Marg hoped she was right. Could Kendrick overcome the shame of admitting to not having the wealth he claimed? He bowed his head, clasped his hands together, and spoke in a shaky voice.

"Yes, I really, really need the money. I'm in over my head. This would be a lifesaver." Kendrick couldn't help himself, adding, "Since the market tanked, I lost a fortune. It wasn't my fault."

Marg's reaction was predictable. "That's bullshit, Kendrick. You had no money to begin with. Accept what we're offering with no grandstanding." She didn't have to go any further. It was widely acknowledged that no one could humiliate Kendrick. Except one thing.

"Sandra would be well taken care of, wouldn't she?" His eyes grew moist, and he had to sit down, overcome with emotion.

Dakari was also overcome. He crossed the room, hauled Kendrick upright, and hugged him like a long-lost brother, tears streaming down his face. By the time he released Kendrick, everyone in the room had tears in their eyes and, spontaneously, they all clapped, louder and louder.

Kendrick quickly recovered.

"What can I say, guys?" he added. "You've just saved my life and my daughter's. Thank you, thank you. You're the best in the world. Nobody would think of this except you guys."

Marg thought it was an over-reaction, bordering on pretence. The other people in the room must have felt the same way. The meeting deteriorated into embarrassment. Mature people shouldn't react emotionally like this, thought Marg. Gail looked at Forest. Dakari looked at Kendrick as if he found a new soulmate.

Gail salvaged the moment.

"I have one question. Where does Rollie fit into this?"

"Rollie? Who cares about Rollie?" asked Marg.

"I really don't care, Marg. But I'm damn curious. Aren't you?"

Chapter 36

Marg was quick to answer, not wanting to return to the love-in she had just witnessed.

"Do you want my opinion about Rollie?"

She put it out as a rhetorical question and then answered her own question.

"In a nutshell, folks, we're looking at an empty vessel, like a barrel rolling down a hill at top speed. Totally out of control."

"I like him, Marg." said Forest. Dakari nodded in agreement. "He's young and a go-getter. How many people his age want to get into politics? He wants to change the world. We need more young people like him."

"Are you sure, Forest? Did Everet ever tell you he suspected Rollie was one of those goons who stormed the Capitol after Trump lost?"

Gail jumped into the conversation.

"Everet mentioned he brought Rollie to Canada to keep him out of trouble. If what Marg says is true, there may be a warrant out for his arrest in the US. I guess the move worked. He's not broken any laws in Canada and been arrested. And if he's that interested in politics, it certainly explains his run for mayor."

Marg continued. "I think it's deeper than that, Gail. Everet must have convinced Rollie to run for mayor. Not only run and be elected, but to also push the sale of the vacant land. I think Rollie is just as complicit as Everet. He's a chip off the old block."

"Well, he's had a master teacher, Marg. In some ways, I wish I knew everything Everet has done. It would be fascinating. Never going to happen now, is it?"

Marg's eyes brightened. Criminals like Everet were familiar territory for her. She made a comment, not directed at anyone. "For sure Everet's slippery. Remember, I told you when we were on our trip, Emile and I found information about Everet that would make your hair curl." She looked directly at Forest, "Excluding you, Forest." Forest absent mindedly rubbed his nearly bald head.

"He's lived by his wits for so long now, I wouldn't put it past him to find a way out. Then again, I've been wrong many times in the past. I hope I'm wrong this time." She flashed a big smile. "Just kidding, folks."

Dakari, observing the hard look on her face, didn't think she was kidding. He spoke up, the only one in the group who made the connection.

"So what's going to happen to Rollie? Do you think the crime guys are going to go after him, too?"

"Of course they are," volunteered Emile. "He's one of the family, Everet's family. These people don't make family distinctions between who's in and who's out. Of course, that isn't the only thing Rollie has to worry about."

Forest thought that running from the mob was more than sufficient to be worried about. What now?

Emile continued. "Rollie has set the town on a course of downsizing our municipal government. I think it may be a tie about who is more angry–the bad guys or the citizens of Port Detour. Rollie has been mayor for four months now and he's lucky. Just wait until someone's house burns down or Philip's Convenience Store is robbed. Will there be enough firemen or police? If I were Rollie, that would be the more scary threat. People will be sorry they elected him and there are going to be a lot of angry citizens, way more than the mob guys. Just imagine an army of angry people coming after him."

He turned to Kendrick, who had remained silent throughout the entire conversation. Marg thought, it's his nephew we're talking about. Why doesn't he say something?

"Kendrick, if I were you, I'd be watching my backside."

Kendrick's face expressed surprise. "But I did nothing! Why would anyone come after me?"

"For one thing, Everet's your brother. Maybe someone on the other side thinks that if Everet doesn't give back the money, you're next on the give list. Maybe they assume you're close to your brother and he's given you the money for safekeeping."

Kendrick seemed to shrink in front of the group.

"No, no, he didn't. You've got to believe me. Marg's got all the money, you know that."

Emile grinned. "Right now, the mob doesn't know that, do they?"

Kendrick's eyes opened wide as the possibility dawned on him. "I guess so, Emile. Do you think I should be worried?"

Emile looked directly at him. He grunted one syllable. "Duh?"

He continued. "I'm also hearing other news about Rollie. I think he may have more trouble than even he's aware of."

Now it was Marg's turn to be surprised. Her brow furrowed as Emile expanded his comment.

"The police guys heard rumours that people are talking about using violence."

Kendrick welcomed the change of subject and quickly jumped in. "Yeah, that's what I've heard at the tavern. Nobody wants to admit they made a voting mistake, but it's there. Between you and me, I heard two guys also talking about lynching him."

Emile immediately asked. "How serious was the conversation, Kendrick? Do you know the guys?"

"I think they were just venting, really only putting it out as the type of threat you hear people make when they're mad or want to be shocking."

Emile looked at him with narrowed eyes. "Are you sure?"

Kendrick's brow wrinkled, and he pulled at the base of his neck, squeezing the loose skin far too long.

"No. People think the kid's crazy and doesn't know the harm he could cause. One guy at the tavern told us he had been mugged and all the police did was make a note of it. No action."

A thought came into Kendrick's mind. Who would protect him if he was in trouble? What if Emile was right? He had an awful thought. Maybe he, deep down, also wanted Rollie to be lynched and removed from office?

"Do you think I should warn Rollie?" he asked to no one in particular.

Marg sighed and repeated Emile's earlier comment. "Duh?"

The conversation opportunities now seemed to be exhausted, and the group got up from their seats and everyone moved to the door and said their good-by's. Kendrick, before he opened his car door, he pulled out his cell phone and made a call.

"Hi Rollie. It's your uncle. We need to talk."

Kendrick listened for a moment. "No, it can't wait. I'll see you at city hall." There was a pause. "Yes, I know it's late, but it's best if no one sees us together."

For the first time in his life, Kendrick had planned ahead.

Chapter 37

Marg's cell phone rang. The caller's name didn't show up on the display and Marg hesitated to answer the unknown number. Maybe it was important, she persuaded herself, and curiosity overcame caution. She punched the accept button.

"So, Marg, I hope you understood my message," came the words from the speaker.

Such drama, thought Marg. Everet was neither smart nor subtle. It didn't take a genius to figure out who took the shot at her.

"Not really. Do you understand it yourself, Everet?"

"What do you mean? Next time you're dead."

"Kind of leaves you in an awkward position, Everet. Dead people can't sign documents. Looks like the money would be gone."

There was a significant pause on the other end. "There must be somebody else."

"No, Everet, there isn't. You'll have to con somebody to raise the missing money. Shouldn't be a problem for you."

There was a pause, as if Everet was trying to digest the message he was receiving.

"Do your worst, Everet. But before you do, you should be aware I have the names and contact info of your so-called business partners. I'm sure they would like to know where they can find you. And your son."

"You don't have a clue where I am, Marg."

"You're right, I don't. But my good friend Emile does. You remember him? The law guy? They know where you are, Everet, and the only reason you haven't been arrested is lack of proof about trying to shoot an innocent citizen. I'm sure your mob friends don't give a hoot about those niceties."

Again there was a pause, a longer one.

"Emile was thinking about contacting them. Are you Ok with that?"

"Marg, there's no need for that. Why are you busting my balls over this? You don't need the money, right? Why not return it and let bygones be bygones?"

Now it was Marg's turn for a pause. She waited a good minute.

"Marg, are you still there?" came Everet's voice over the speaker. Marg could detect a slight tremor in his voice.

"Let bygones be bygones, eh? That's an admirable thought, Everet. But I have some problems with that. There's the case of the rape. There's also an attempt to run me down. And I love the latest. You want to shoot me, but not to kill me, only maim. Isn't that right?"

"Fuck you, Marg. I've changed my mind. You're as good as dead. If I'm going down, so are you."

"Slight problem, Everet. Remember the advice I gave you?"

"No, I don't, but it doesn't matter."

"My advice then, and now, is for you to run, Everet. Run as fast as you can and as far away as you can. You're disposable. Nobody will care about another mob killing, least of all if it's you. My last piece of advice? Why don't you contact Rey Rey Gonsalves? He knows all about funerals. Goodbye, Everet."

"I'm coming after you, Marg,"

"Everet, you've got bigger problems than coming after me. I'm hanging up now. Knowing you has been one of the worst experiences of my life. Goodbye and good riddance. The world won't miss you."

Marg found the entire conversation strangely satisfying. It was as if a weight had been lifted from her shoulders. It was something she needed after so many years of feeling ashamed. There was no need to tell Emile about the conversation. This was only for her.

Her cell phone rang. Again, Marg didn't recognize the incoming call number. She took a chance. The last time had proven it sometimes was worth answering unknown callers.

"Hello," she answered tentatively.

"I want to speak to Margie. Are you her?" said a hoarse voice with a Brooklyn accent.

"You must have the wrong number. Who's calling?"

"Naw, I got the right number. It's Julius."

Chapter 38

Marg was furiously trying to recall anyone she knew who had the name Jules. One thing she knew from her criminal defence days were the odd names of many of the people she was defending. Jules certainly fit that category. The dots suddenly connected.

The caller continued talking. "You can call me Jules. Now do you remember? You got Freddie and Mario off."

She defended Freddie and Mario years ago in Toronto. They worked for a man named Jules Castellano, an American, who claimed he was a real estate investor. Spike's notes confirmed Everet was laundering money for organized crime, specifically the mob from Syracuse. Now that she knew the name of Everet's client and it took little brainpower to figure out that she had come into possession of Jules Castellano's money. No doubt Everet, wanting to save his own skin, told Jules that Marg had his money and wouldn't give it back.

"Is that you, Mr. Castellano? The gentleman I did some work for a few years back?"

"Yeah, same guy, Margie. I don't think I ever thanked you for getting Freddie and Mario off. You did a hell of a job for those goombahs. You earned your fee on that one, considering what they did. They almost killed my excellent reputation in Toronto."

"Not that I'm really interested, just curious. Where are they now?"

"Ah, we moved them to another side of the business. As negotiators, they sucked. Now they're doing what they're good at."

Marg decided not to touch that one. But Jules was in a talkative mood and, for some reason, felt Marg had to understand what happened.

"When you're an investor like me, you have to be subtle. You don't want to drive up the price, ya know, real estate owners are fickle. They think their property is always worth more than it really is. Freddie and Mario tried to explain the facts of life to the building owner. They were just unlucky with what happened."

Marg didn't share the view the two 'goombahs', as Jules called them, were unlucky.

"If I remember correctly, there was some question just how the owner broke his leg. All I did was show the jury the height of the step Mr. Chen tripped down. Nobody pushed him. Your guys were innocent. It was pure harassment."

"Yeah, yeah, whatever. You did a great job. I assume my accountant paid you. I never heard back."

"Sure did, sir. You were most generous. You really didn't have to give the bonus."

"I know, I know. But you didn't turn it down, did you, sweetheart?"

Hearing the challenge, Marg stiffened, pursed her lips, and replied. "I never look a gift horse in the mouth, sir. Anyway, how did you track me down? You know I'm retired, right? "

"Not from what I hear, Margie. Everet tells me you're holding something for me right now. Sounds to me like you're still working."

"You hear wrong Mr. Castellano. I live in a small town now and the most work I do is walking the dog and my hobby is watching for anything illegal at city hall. If you need a lawyer, I can recommend some very good ones."

"Margie, you're a smart counsellor. Let's not waste time. I want you to hear a story and then tell me what I should do. OK?"

Marg mulled things over in her mind. It was one thing for Everet to know she would not return the money, but it was an entirely different playing field if Mr. Big was leading the team.

All she could do was say, "OK."

"Good girl," said Jules. "If you didn't know it before, you know it now. Everet Overland is an associate of mine. For the past two years, Everet has arranged some investments for me, great investments. When he said he had a good real estate opportunity in Canda, I got interested. Somehow he found out that a two-bit town named Port Detour had some valuable property and Everet knew how to buy it dirt cheap. I liked his plan, creative you know, and he also spreads the risk by getting his son involved. I liked the kid and thought they made a great team. His name's Rollie."

"I know him, Jules. Smooth talker, that one."

"You're right. Margie. Could be an expert con man like his father, but he'd have to buy some smarts first. Not the sharpest knife in the drawer."

Her thoughts, completely.

Jules continued.

"Anyway, I send him five mill and then he tells me he bought the property. He left out a small part. I sent him five mill but I hear that the property only cost two mill. Where's the other three mill? I call him on it. Now he's dancing. He tried to send back the three mill, but guess what? He says you handled all the money and the legals and won't give it back. You know what I think?"

Marg's brain alarm went off. Everet had tried to pull off a big con of the one person no one should cross.

"What did you think, Jules?"

Jules' voice lowered and he spoke slowly. "Margie, the guy was going to rip me off. If I didn't hear the sale was for two mill, Everet just might be walking around with three mill in his pocket. Now I hear it's you who has the money. Are you and Everet working me over, Margie?"

Blood drained from her face, and her mouth turned dry. She immediately recalled her thoughts when she was asked by the Blue Duck group if they were in any danger. Of course not, she had pronounced. She lied, but compensated by telling herself she would think of a solution if it happened. It was now time to think.

She chose her words carefully.

"Had I known it was you, Mr. Castellano, we wouldn't be having this conversation. I respect you. It's Everet Overland, sir. He's the one I'm after."

"Margie, I told you, drop the Mister, it's Jules. What could Everet Overland do to you that you need to go after him? The guy's a nobody, a weasel. You're a smart lady. You got better things to do."

If there was ever time for the truth, it was now, thought Marg. Anyway, she had already shared her story with everybody. It wasn't as though it was a secret. But the tremors in her voice were easily detected. She spoke rapidly, as if talking quickly would diminish the effect the rape had on her entire life.

"Everet raped me when I was a teenager, Jules."

"What?" Jules' voice came over the phone in a higher pitch. "You gotta be kidding. And you didn't do nothing for all those years? What's with you Margie?"

"You wouldn't understand, Jules. It was traumatic. Lifestyle traumatic."

"Oh, I understand. Big tough guy beats up and abuses a woman. What's to understand? Guys like him don't last long in my social circle. We get them out real quick."

Marg understood. And it wasn't just in or out. Out meant out, finished, caput.

Jules wasn't finished. "So, he got a free out of jail ticket from you. Didn't you even want revenge? What kind of upbringing did you have?"

Marg couldn't rationalize her response. Or even her comfort in talking to Jules. She could never do this with her father, and her mother was totally unsympathetic. She knew her hardness came from her mother. Her father was a weakling, forever under his wife's thumb. The words came tumbling out without restraint.

"Oh. I wanted revenge, Jules. I wanted it badly. But, tell me, how does a lawyer get revenge and if she's caught, keep her job? I've waited a long time for the chance, Jules, believe me. Do you want to know what I thought my revenge might be?"

"Shoot, sugar."

"The only way I can get some revenge is to not let him get the three million dollars. That's where you come in. You're my revenge, Jules. I didn't know it was you, but it didn't matter. You and your associates know what to do when somebody crosses you. That's what I hoped would happen."

"What about the three mill, Margie? You telling me you don't need or want it?"

"Stop calling me Margie. It's Marg. As to the three mill, you may find it hard to believe, I don't need or want the money. But I have a use for it, a good use."

There was a long pause on Jules' end of the phone. Marg thought maybe the connection was lost.

"Margie, I believe you. You got class, not like that sleazebag. You can't make up a thing like that. Not only does he try to rip me off, you're telling me he's a, what's the word, predator? He beats up women? In my world, that's a big no-no. We don't have none of that in my organization. The matter is settled."

"What do you mean, settled?"

"You don't want to know, counsellor."

But Marg knew. Was she now the accomplice to a crime? What if his or her phones were tapped?

"I said, don't worry Margie. Anyway, I know a real good criminal lawyer if it goes south." Marg heard this throaty laugh on the other end of the phone. "Lighten up, Margie. Nothing will happen. At least to you." Another loud laugh.

His voice turned low. "Let's get serious. When do I get my money back?"

"As soon as you give me instructions where to send it, Jules."

Marg thought of the promise she had made to Kendrick. What about his daughter? Why had she let her mouth run off like that? Well, she hadn't been a lawyer for forty years without knowing how to get out of awkward situations. She'd figure something out.

"That's a problem, Margie. You can't send it back to me. We can't afford to have it traced."

"Then it's mine?"

Marg was instantly relieved when she heard the deep laugh. Jules thought it was funny.

"I didn't say that, Margie. All I said, it was a problem. Anyway, you're the mouthpiece. You gotta have ideas. Let's hear what you come up with."

"OK. Give me a day. Give me your number, I'll call and we can meet. You are in Canada, aren't you?"

"I'm somewhere, Margie, and no, I won't give you my number. It changes, anyway. I'll call tomorrow and we'll set something up."

Marg pressed the end call button and immediately thoughts of regret filled her head. She always prided herself on making calm, cool decisions using all the information available. What had she got herself into? Had she had completely ignored her lifelong standards and also jeopardized her reason for being in Port Detour?

Chapter 39

Someone had once asked her, "Why here, Marg? Why Port Detour to retire to?"

"Because it's quiet and pretty and stable. Nothing much happens in Port Detour, which suits me to a T," she had replied. Toronto had nothing for her. She had few friends and the city was for a young person's lifestyle. She craved a social life, small town friendly and no pretensions. Just plain, nice people in a pretty setting.

Until now. Late last night, she made a decision to get involved with an organized crime individual. Not that she was a criminal. Far from it, but to actually be partners? Let's wait, she decided over breakfast, until Jules heard about her idea and made his decision.

She had to laugh about herself. Not a criminal? She had suckered the Overland brothers into parting with three million dollars. Age kind of blurs the boundaries.

Marg got the call at eleven AM.

"Well?" said the now recognizable voice. "What have you got?"

"I got lots, Jules, but we need to meet. It's a beautiful day, so how about outside? Are you available in the afternoon, say two o'clock? Where are you, anyway?"

Her mind was working at light-speed, possibilities rippling through her head. She knew it was naïve to think nothing bad could happen outside. In fact, it could be the opposite. Maybe I'm too paranoid?

I've dealt with this type of person all my life. Why start worrying now? But just how close should she get to this man?

The deep voice laughed again. "You don't need to know, sweetheart. Just tell me where. If it's Port Detour, I can be there in thirty minutes. I'm driving."

She gave him directions, which he didn't question. GPS, she surmised, and thirty minutes meant he must be in or near the town.

At two o'clock, Marg sat at a picnic table in Carter Park. The park was one of twenty in Port Detour but was the smallest and little used. Marg thought it was the prettiest, with mature maples, oaks, and evergreens interspersed with flowering shrubs. The park was sited on the stony waterfront of Lake Ontario, bounded on the east side by Dale Creek and a line of evergreens on the west, the other side the start of the Blue Duck Tavern parking lot. From her vantage spot, she could see the plywood Blue Duck sign on the roof but little else of the tavern.

The current situation reminded her of a crime TV show, unfolding in weekly episodes. Organized crime, money laundering, illegal land sales, mysterious gaps in peoples' lives, her revelations about a matter of forty years ago. Even Emile Bartlet. That brought a smile to her face until she heard the sound of an approaching car.

She looked north toward the small parking lot and saw a black Cadillac drive in and stop against the parking lot markers. It was a couple of years old and the licence plates which identified it as a

New York vehicle. The licence plate holder said it was purchased from a car dealer in Syracuse. The driver got out and, without hesitation, walked directly towards the picnic bench. Marg couldn't believe her eyes. Jules couldn't have been more than five foot six, but it was his face that set him apart. Al Capone sans the spats, white fedora, and a cigar.

He waved, called out "Hi Margie," and moved to the picnic bench. Marg, based on his thinning grey hair, judged his age to be mid-fifties. A broad smile on his face and eyes in direct contact with her seemed to be permission for him to sit down opposite her.

Marg gestured and said, "Have a seat, Jules. Any trouble finding the place?"

"Naw, I knew where it was. So, what have you got, Margie?"

She gave up. Margie it was.

For a first time meeting, he was decidedly uninterested in her. No 'how are you?' or 'why are you in Port Detour? Not even 'do you like dogs or cats?' Just, 'what you got, Margie?' She got the message. The less people knew about Jules, the better he felt.

"Jules, you just made a real estate investment. That's smart. I know another one that is even better. It would be a perfect investment with the money you have left over. Three million, right?"

"So far, so good, counsellor," he laughed.

"I'm not an investment advisor, but I handle my own investments. Besides real estate, do you know the next best investment?"

"No I don't, honey. All I know is how to make it, not how to invest it. I need a retirement fund, that's what I need. Something legit, you know."

"Health care is where it's at, Jules. Enormous demand, a lot of government support and it always involves real estate."

"Yeah, I know. I like real estate. It never goes away like some other shit I've been involved with. And you can't trust those financial advisors, Margie. Look at Everet. Anyway, you're talking about the three mill, right?"

"Yes, Jules. And another three mill."

Marg could see Jules bristle. "You want another three mill? What do you take me for Margie?"

"It's not what you think, Jules. Let me explain."

Jules moved to the edge of his seat and leaned in closer to Marg. She explained about Evergreen Gardens, what it was and where it was located. In her usual logical and organized fashion, she summarized the financial situation the home found itself in.

"Jules, there's something else."

"There always is, babe. Shoot."

Marg explained her idea about the Blue Duck Charitable Trust. Jules listened without saying a word. Suddenly he grinned. Marg continued.

"So, you see Jules, it'll take three mill to set up the Blue Duck Charitable Trust and another three mill to pay off the mortgage. Then it's yours one hundred percent. My idea could result in a big return on the money invested."

"Let me think, Marg. Real estate, government support, lots of old people, great turnover. Must be a good return on my money, right? And you've got financial statements I can look at?"

Marg realized Jules wasn't a slow, dim-witted thug. He was a smart businessman.

"You're sharp, Jules." Jules beamed. Marg continued. "You're right. After the mortgage is paid off, I estimate an investor would get twenty, twenty-five per cent on their investment."

"So all I got to do is ship three mill here?" He looked off into the sky and then swung his gaze back to Marg. "OK, smart lady. If I do that, you gonna guarantee I get twenty percent?"

"Yeah, sure," said Marg. "And pigs can fly. Get real Jules."

"Just testing, Margie, just testing. I like this idea. Ya wanna know why?"

Did she have a choice?

"Real estate, Margie, and more. You don't know me, but this isn't bullshit. I got a younger brother. He's in a home in Syracuse, a dump, Margie, a dump. But I can't find anything better. Zane is retarded. Nice kid, I love him to death, but he can't take care of himself. Who's gonna take care of him after I'm gone?"

"Zane? His name is Zane?"

"Yeah, my Ma was a big fan of westerns. Books, movies, TV shows, that was Ma. You know that writer, a guy called Zane Grey? That was my mother's favourite. Boy, could he ever write good westerns. My brother is named after him." Jules had tears in his eyes and didn't seem at all embarrassed.

"You picked a nice place to meet Margie. Why here?"

"It's quiet and peaceful, Jules. I need that after my life in Toronto."

"Yeah, I can understand that. It's time for me, too." He looked around, hearing the waves lap on the shore and the birds chattering in the trees.

"How about a beer, Margie?" he said as he pointed to the Blue Duck sign. "Looks like a good place there. We can sit outside."

"On two conditions, Jules."

"What's that?"

"First, are you going to let me create the Blue Duck Charitable Trust with your money and invest five mill in Evergreen Gardens? We could pay off the mortgage."

"That's three mill, Margie, not five. What's the matter with your memory?" He laughed his throaty laugh. "Good try, counsellor. Let me think about it. What's the other condition?"

"Why do you insist on calling me Margie? My name is Marg."

He got up and started walking to the tavern. Marg also wanted to know about Everet's future, but didn't want to interrupt Jules thinking about Evergreen Gardens. Oh, well, perhaps a beer would loosen his lips. She got up and hastened to join him - Jules was moving with some speed towards the watering hole. As she approached him, he turned around and extended his hand, then grabbed her hand and led the way to the tavern.

Chapter 40

Jules graciously held the front door of the Blue Duck open. They walked across the room, now lit in late afternoon sunlight. Passing the bar, she slowed and said, "Good afternoon, Kendrick. Where is everybody? It's empty here."

"Most afternoon we're busy, but not today. Maybe it's the weather. It's nicer outside than in. Why don't you sit outside on the deck?"

She led the way through the sliding glass doors and chose a table as far away from the rest of the empty tables as possible. Again, Jules graciously held out a chair for her.

"That's Everet's brother, Margie?" He pointed to the bar area.

She nodded yes. He continued, "Good, wouldn't want him to be confused with his brother. Wouldn't that be embarrassing?" He continued to look at Kendrick, no doubt making doubly sure he knew the difference between the two brothers, thought Marg.

"Do you think I should ask him where Everet and the kid are?"

"I'd let it die for now, Jules. No, no, that's not what it sounds like. I really think you should let a sleeping dog lie. I'm sure you have other ways to find someone."

"Yeah, you're right. Anyway, what'll you have?" Kendrick was now standing in front of them, looking for their order.

"Got any Sam Adams?" Kendrick nodded yes and looked at Marg. "I'll have a Steam Whistle, Kendrick." Their beers were on the table in minutes, not even enough time to start a conversation. Jules took a long look at Kendrick, to the point of embarrassment.

Marg broke the silence. "This here is a good friend of mine. Kendrick, meet Jules. Jules is from the states, just visiting." She let it die, but Kendrick didn't make any move to extend the conversation. He nodded and went back to the bar.

"OK Jules, time to own up. What's with calling me Margie? Where's that coming from?"

For the first time, Marg saw hesitation and an immediate loss for words from Jules. She gave him a quiet time until he spoke. He blurted out what must have been building inside him.

"My wife died two years ago. Her name was Margie and you wouldn't believe how closely you sound and look like her. You two could have been twins."

"I'm so sorry, Jules. I think you must miss her a lot if you can't help calling me Margie." An awful thought occurred to her, which luckily Jules got to first.

"Don't get me wrong, Marg. I could easily say 'I love you' right now, but death is final. You can't recreate what's gone. That's all I want to say. End of conversation."

Time to shut up, she thought. Let's change to something else.

"I appreciate that, Jules. You appear to be a gentleman, real old school. I love that. But I have to tell you, calling me Margie is a little ghoulish, don't you think?"

Not knowing what else to do, Marg took a large gulp of her beer. Strangely, Jules did exactly the same thing, as if neither one wanted to further confront the issue.

Despite saying 'end of conversation', it wasn't really the end. Jules needed to talk.

"Yeah, you're right, Marg. Don't think I haven't thought of that. We had forty great years together, but I can't seem to let go. You were like a dream come true. Margie was back. Except she isn't. OK, enough of Margie. You're Marg and that's your name. Let's use it."

"OK with me, Jules. I've used it all my life. It seems to work. Now, what about the care facility?"

"God dammit, Marg. It's only been fifteen minutes since we talked about it. Enough, already. I'll let you know when I've decided. Right now, let's talk about Marg. You're from Port Detour is all I know. Fill me in."

Two beers later, Jules seemed to be 'filled in'.

"Pretty impressive for a small-town girl, Marg. Why didn't you ever get married?"

"You're the only one I've ever told this to, Jules. The experience I went thorough with Everet affected my life and what I thought about men. That's why."

"That's bullshit, Marg, and you know it. It's a great excuse for you. It happened forty years ago and didn't seem to stop you from being a successful mouthpiece. You never confronted him, did you, until recently? How do you feel now that you did?"

"I've got a boyfriend, Jules. That's progress. Want to know something else? The idea of getting revenge isn't what it's cracked up to be. Sure, I wish he were dead, but that's just to protect future victims. Me? I don't feel any better. Who cares what happens to him? He's a loser. Since I've been back to Port Detour, I've got my life back. And I've got Emile, I think."

"Emile? That's the boyfriend. What's he do, Marg?"

"He's a retired cop, Jules. Careful what you say," she laughed.

Jules forced a grin. The conversation had stopped. The beer glasses were empty. They retraced their steps to Jules' car.

"I'll call you tomorrow, Marg. I gotta think about what you told me about the investment. One thing. Being partners with you is a bonus."

Chapter 41

Jules' call came late in the day.

"Is that you, Marg?"

"Yes, Jules. It's the number you dialled."

"Perfect. We're good to go. We're partners now."

There was silence on Marg's end. This was too easy. Was he serious or leading her on?

"Marg, are you there?"

"Yes, I'm here, Jules. That's great news. What made up your mind?"

"You did, Marg. In the last two years, I got my eyes opened. Did you know everyone wants to marry Jules? You should have heard what some of those broads told me, to say nothing of what they offered. I never knew you could do such things. But you, you were different."

"What do you mean, different?"

"You were upfront about what you wanted and it wasn't even for you. You're one of a kind, Marg. No, wrong, you're two of a kind. My Margie was number one."

"Why thanks, Jules. I really appreciate that. And you're right. You and I could make an enormous difference in a lot of lives."

"But I have two conditions, counsellor."

Here comes the catch, thought Marg. As if being in business with a mob boss wasn't enough reason for a lawyer to run away. "Shoot."

"Condition number one, Marg. The name of the home has to be changed. I want it called Sophie's House. That was my mother's name, and she welcomed everyone into her home, no questions asked. She was a saint, Marg. This is her legacy."

"I like that, Jules. And number two?"

"You gotta take in my brother, Zane. No discussion."

"Jules, when I get off the phone, I'm in action. We got a purchase to make and papers to sign."

"That's it? What about Zane?"

"You said no discussion, Jules. What else do you want from me? Tell you what, I'll give you my first-born. OK? But don't worry, Zane is in with open arms."

"What do you mean, your first-born? You're into your sixties, Marg,"

"So? You really are a chauvinist, Jules." She could hear the chuckle at the other end of the line. Marg wondered if he really knew the meaning.

"Do your stuff, counsellor. I'll call in a week. I got some other things to take care of."

Marg didn't want to ask. Jules had no such hesitation.

"Yeah, it's a matter of life and death, Marg. You know what I mean?"

Chapter 42

It was bitterly cold and February in Sudbury. Floyd heard his cellphone ring in the next room. It took about a minute to find it, hiding under today's issue of the Sudbury Northerner.

He picked it up and pressed the receive button to hear a familiar voice.

"Guess who, Floyd?"

In his mind's eye, Kendrick envisaged the bungalow next door from Floyd's, his house, his empty bungalow in Sudbury. It had been two years since he was in the house. Floyd watched over it and took care of any maintenance. Nobody wanted to buy or rent it. He was sure organized crime had no interest in Sudbury.

Floyd listened to his ex-neighbour for a few minutes and ended the conversation with, "Sure, Kendrick, no problem. Just have the kid come to my house and I'll give him the keys. He'll be here Friday, right? You said his name was Rollie? He'll have to shovel the driveway and the walk. You never paid me to do that, remember?"

Rollie showed up Friday afternoon, parked his ten-year-old Honda on the road in front of Floyd's house, got out and left the engine running, wheezing and groaning in the cold air. If Floyd wasn't home, he had concerns about starting the engine in sub-zero weather. A few minutes later he returned to the car, grabbed a duffel bag, turned off the engine and waded through the knee deep snow to the front door. Hopefully, his safe house was safe. Who would want to go to Sudbury in the middle of winter? He turned up the thermostat.

Six months later, Floyd, in number thirty-six, yelled across the twenty-foot gap to its twin, number thirty-eight. The late August sun beat down on both backyard decks in a final glorious goodbye to summer.

Each bungalow sported a worn rear deck with a small set of stairs going down to the open backyard. It extended as a small piece of lawn before running into grey rocks rising out of the ground. The rocks continued their rise, turning into a thirty foot high hill, populated with an occasional poplar and pine tree or small shrub. The view wasn't pretty.

"Hey Rollie, you want a beer? C'mon over."

Rollie Overland sat on a well-worn lawn chair on the deck of number thirty-eight, reading an illustrated book. The invitation was timely. The book was boring.

"Be right over," he yelled back. He almost ran down the stairs to the backyard, across the scrabbly lawn, and up Floyd's steps to be greeted with an open can of beer thrust his way.

"Sit down, kid, enjoy the view," the older man laughed. "I talked to your uncle Kendrick yesterday. Your uncle wanted to know how you were. Do you young guys ever hear about keeping in touch with your relatives?"

"Yeah, I've been busy." Rollie took a long swig of his beer. "Floyd, you wouldn't believe the trouble I've had getting work. I've had more odd jobs than a tool at the Rent-All. Doesn't anyone work full-time here?"

"So what's the surprise, kid? I told your uncle Kendrick when he called in the winter, that jobs were scarce. Didn't he tell you?"

"He didn't tell me much, Floyd, other than he owned an empty house in Sudbury that nobody wanted to buy or rent. Anyway, I had little choice. Things happened pretty fast in Port Detour. Who would have thought?"

Floyd's interest level rose to new heights. Kendrick hadn't told him anything about the kid and why he wanted to come to Sudbury. Rollie's statement about things happening fast was like honey to a bear. Retired people live on gossip. What else was there to do?

"Good thing I ran into those friends of your uncle, eh? I guess they all made it home safely. Didn't hear from them until your uncle called. What was going on down there? It sounded a little mysterious."

"No mystery, Floyd. Everyone knows the story, what with me being mayor and all."

Floyd could barely contain himself. The kid was the Mayor of Port Detour?

"You know what happened, don't you, Floyd?"

Floyd shook his head so rapidly his Blue Jay's cap nearly fell off. Rollie's eyes registered surprise.

"Don't you read the papers and watch news on TV, Floyd?"

"No. Why would I? You can't believe anything you hear, or even see, these days. Everyone lies, you know." He leaned back, crossed his arms, a smug look on his face as if lack of knowledge was a badge of honour.

Rollie had seen that attitude before. It was what got him elected mayor of Port Detour. People will believe anything as long as it agrees with their views. Promising to lower taxes and reduce services in Port Detour had struck a chord.

"So what happened in Port Detour, Rollie? You're no longe the mayor, right?"

"Right, Floyd, even though I delivered what I said I would. Nobody liked it, except for the land sale. And I got taxes down by fifty per cent."

"We need you here," said Floyd. "Why don't you run for mayor?"

Rollie closed his eyes to purge any image of such a happening.

"But what didn't they like, kid?"

"They didn't like me reducing the size of the police, fire, public works departments. They didn't care about eliminating the Parks and Recreation, though. But I was harassed everywhere I went and even got beat up by a bunch of mothers."

Rollie opened another can of beer and took a long swig.

"Then a mob of taxpayers came after me. It was nearly four months after I was elected, and at least a hundred of them charged into the council chambers with a rope and a noose."

"Hard to believe, kid. So you got elected Mayor, then got rid of the police, fire, maintenance and parks departments. No wonder they came after you. Pardon the thought, but why did you do such a stupid thing?"

Rollie recoiled.

"It wasn't stupid, Floyd. I got taxes down by over fifty per cent. And I didn't get rid of those departments. I only reduced them."

"Whatever. Did the mob ever catch you? You said they had a hangman's noose."

"Not a chance. I got out the back door, ran through the parking lot and didn't stop running until I got to my uncle Kendrick's house. That's when he made the call to you. Good thing. Those crazies showed up at uncle Kendrick's door an hour later, looking for me."

"What did they want, son? You were the Mayor, not a criminal."

Rollie's next comment almost caused him to drop his beer. Recovering, he chugged the whole can.

"Not according to them. I later heard they were pissed about somebody's house burning down and the bank being robbed. I might have gone too far. We only had a few policemen and firefighters left and they were on strike, objecting to the cuts." He repeated his favourite saying. "Who would have thought?"

The kid's a nutcase, thought Floyd. Personality plus, but no brains. He recalled some crazy incidents over the past forty years that Kendrick was responsible for. The nut doesn't fall far from the tree, he concluded.

"Yeah, but there's more to it, isn't there? Your uncle warned me to keep quiet and not let anyone know you were here. He was wild, Rollie, wild. He sounded scared and out of control. What's really going on? Did you kill someone?"

Rollie stared off into the rock hill. His lips quavered as he wrestled with something in his mind. Finally, he turned to Floyd.

"I gotta tell someone, Floyd. It's eating me inside."

It all tumbled out without regard for consequences. The run for mayor at his father's request, the sale of land to a numbered company, his father's involvement with organized crime and the demand to return the three million excess funds.

"How do you know all this, Rollie? That's not something anyone would want known. Who told you?"

"I got a call from my dad just before that last council meeting. He wanted to meet me and explain. I had no idea what he was talking about, but we met at the coffee shop and he talked for a long time."

"That's smart," interjected Floyd. "Great place for a private talk. Now I know where the stupid part of this story comes from."

Rollie ignored the shot and continued.

"Dad had just come from a meeting at that artist guy's house, a guy name Dakari. He was scared, Floyd, scared out of his wits. He told me everything, including how Marg O'Toole wasn't giving the money back. Right then he knew he was a marked man."

"Whoa, Rollie. Who's Marg O'Toole?"

"Give me another beer, Floyd. This'll take a long time to tell."

Indeed, it did. It took two additional beers and more than an hour to provide Floyd with all the details.

Floyd, sitting on his backyard deck, three hundred kilometres north of sin city, Toronto, had a hard time grasping the reality of it. Organized crime? A marked man? Did Floyd know too much, now? Were they going to come after him?

Rollie threw the last empty can on the lawn and reached into Floyd's cooler for another Bud.

"Floyd, you can't tell any of this to anyone, OK?"

Disappointment swept over Floyd. "Why not?" he frowned, as he asked.

"That organized crime gang is now looking for me. I'm pretty sure they think I'm involved with hiding their money and they'll come after me if they know where I live. "

"That's a stretch, Rollie. You had nothing to do with what your father did. Don't exaggerate, it's not healthy."

"You don't understand, Floyd. I'm family and according to them, everybody in a family is guilty."

Floyd didn't look convinced.

"Floyd, I bet you watch some Netflix crime series and also some gangster movies, right?"

"Yeah, so what?"

"Who gets killed, Floyd? Do the guys with guns say to their enemies, I won't shoot you or you until they get to one person and they put a bullet in their head and then say to the next person, you can go?"

"I see your point," said Floyd, now with his hand in the cooler to grab another beer. "I get the picture. Mum's the word. Anyway, I assume you won't be staying here for long, will you?" The less time he was near Rollie, the better.

"No, this is perfect. Anyway, it's good to be living next door to a hunter. You got the guns to protect me in case they show up, right? I've seen you practice your target shooting right from this very porch."

Rollie brightened at the thought, a grin on his face. He raised his arms in imitation of shooting a rifle, loudly said bang and downed his beer. He put the imaginary rifle down, gazed off, and studied the rock hill, opened another beer, and then stood up and started pacing. At the little stairway, he turned and faced Floyd.

"I gotta tell you one more thing, Floyd." Suddenly, his eyes filled with tears and he started sobbing uncontrollably. Floyd had only seen one other man cry in his life. His father mourned his mother's passing with exactly the same display.

"Floyd, I'm sure my dad is dead. They killed him. I havn't heard from him in over six months and he doesn't answer his cell."

Floyd was rigid and didn't know what to say. He felt sorry for the young man, but his worst fears were realized. He could be the innocent bystander caught in the cross-fire.

The only thing he could do was commiserate. "Sit down, kid, and tell me all about it."

Rollie composed himself, took a sip of his beer and sat down facing Floyd. The sun continued to beat down, warm and bright, in direct contrast to the dark story Rollie was telling. Floyd thought it should be raining, or at least overcast, to fit the tale.

"Right after I left Port Detour, I got a call from my Dad. He was really down. He wanted to say goodbye. I asked where he was going, but I didn't twig onto the meaning of what he was telling me."

"What do you mean?"

"He was talking in riddles, Floyd. Talking about going home when he was already in Port Detour, or at least that was where I assumed he was. He talked about his life and how he had screwed up and made a big point talking about his organized crime acquaintances."

"What about them?"

"He claimed they were after him in a terrible way. Bad, as in, they wanted to kill him if they didn't get their money back."

"Didn't he tell them about this Marg keeping all the money?"

"Yeah, but they didn't believe him. Anyway, Marg has a policeman as a close friend. That didn't go down well with Dad's associates. They accused him of lying. They also said that unless he came up with the three mill in one week, he might not see the light of day for much longer. That's the last I heard from him. I'm scared, Floyd. He's gone missing before, but always stayed in contact."

Floyd seemed to daydream, if only for a few seconds. His mind appeared to be elsewhere, and his comment provided no comfort to Rollie.

"I can't help you, kid. Sorry."

Chapter 43

Rollie finally had a job. Driving a delivery truck wasn't much, but at least it was enough to pay the bills and the occasional case of beer. So far, Rollie's grasp for the brass ring of life far exceeded his reach. His conversation with Floyd a few weeks ago about his affairs and his missing father brought some peace to his mind. But he still missed him.

The cold weather in February was now forgotten. The summer was glorious, except for the mosquitos. The September weather had been spectacular, and this Saturday was no different. He hauled his worn deck chair out from under the deck and sat down facing the sun. He just sat there, reading nothing, drinking nothing, just taking in the sun's rays. He didn't know anyone in Sudbury and had to admit he was lonely. His limited financial resources almost dictated a hermit's life. But at least he was safe.

He dozed off and in a sleepy haze, thought he heard some feet climb the short stairway from the back lawn. Suddenly aware of why he was there, he opened his eyelids just enough to see, but not enough to alert the intruder.

The voice startled him.

"Hi son, whatcha up to?"

He was dreaming.

"Didn't you hear me, Rollie? It's your Dad."

Rollie bounded out of his chair and stood right in front of his father. Everet was dressed in worker clothes - blue jeans, work boots and a light windbreaker. He carried a small travel bag, the worse for wear.

He dropped the bag and put his arms around Rollie. "It's great to see you, Rollie."

Tears streamed down the young man's face. He said nothing and returned the hug, hanging on for a good two minutes.

"It's really you." He repeated, "It's you. What are you doing here? Why are you here? You're alive."

"Damn right I'm alive, son. They can't keep a good man down. What about you?"

They sat on the deck until the sun went down. The reunion talk was non-stop. Rollie was the happiest he had been since arriving in the north.

"How about going out for supper? We can celebrate."

Next door, Floyd made his supper of soup and a small micro-waved pizza. He ate it standing up, gazing out his back window at the grey rock hills beyond his backyard. The sound of another voice next door made him curious. He could see Rollie sitting with an older man, talking animatedly amid much laughter. The man looked familiar. It wasn't his old neighbour Everet, but it might also have been his twin. The face looked older, but the smile and the wavy hair were definitely the same. In fact, Rollie looked like this guy.

Finally, the pin dropped. It must be Everet's brother, Rollie's father. This guy could put a thousand bucks in Floyd's pocket. All it would take is one call.

Floyd looked through the pile of loose papers on the counter. Six months ago, the guy from Toronto had left his number. Where was it?

The small scrap of paper was at the bottom of the pile, the name Mario printed in caps and a Toronto area code number beneath it. He picked up the phone and dialled the number.

"Yeah," was all he heard by whoever answered the phone.

"Is that Mario? It's Floyd Waters, you remember, in Sudbury."

"Yeah, Floyd, whatcha got?"

"Is that offer to let you know if Kendrick Overland or his brother shows up, still open? Will I get my thousand dollars if I see either?"

"Of course, Floyd." Mario's voice had softened. "Have you seen them?

"Kendrick's not here, but his brother is here right now. And he's with his son. They're at Kendrick's house, right next to mine. Do they still owe the money? Is that why you want to know where they are?"

"Big time, Floyd. They owe even more now. We've got to talk to them. How long is this brother staying?"

"I haven't got a clue, Mario. Probably not long. The guy doesn't have any luggage, only a carry-on bag. What do you want me to do?"

"Nothing, Floyd, nothing. I'm coming up to Sudbury right away before the guy leaves. I'll bring your dough with me. See you tomorrow." The call went dead.

They celebrated by going out to Tim Horton's, each ordering chili and a honey glazed donut with a large coffee. Everet was in his glory, telling Rollie how he had evaded whoever was pursuing him, embellishing the story at just the right moments. Finally, the question most on Rollie's mind couldn't be avoided.

"So, Dad, are they still after you?"

Everet looked at his son, hesitating to answer. What could he say? The mob had a long memory, but he had no reason to think they even knew where he was. And he hadn't used his old identity for months.

"Probably, but I know how to cover my tracks, Rollie. I'll tell you, it hasn't been easy and money is scarce, but I think they've lost my trail. I'm back in business. Meet Earl O'Connor, your new best buddy."

He dug into his jeans, pulled out a wallet, and spread the cards on the table. A new Visa, driver's license, birth certificate and health card, all in the name of Earl O'Connor. He held up a Tim Horton's gift card marked $100. "Used once, an hour ago. My treat."

The rest of the evening went by swiftly. Returning home, 'Earl' was settled into a spare bedroom and Rollie didn't see him until near noon the next day.

"Morning, Dad. It's a glorious day. How about lunch on the deck? I made some cheese and ham sandwiches. Do you want a beer with it?"

'Earl' picked up his plate and beer and walked out to the sunlit deck. He sat down at the old picnic table. Rollie sat opposite him.

"I love having you back, Dad. What can we do together?"

Marg and Emile were inseparable. They enjoyed each other's company with over the top enthusiasm. The Blue Duck Charitable Trust was operating, and the Evergreen Gardens purchase was in the final signature stage.

The previous six months had been the happiest Marg ever experienced. She and Emile had gone to restaurants, plays, events, hiked, day tripped and were together most of every day. They rarely missed a meal together.

"Emile, are you happy living in that big old house of yours?" she had asked three months ago.

"Sometimes. Why do you ask Marg? Dolores and I bought that place shortly after we got married. It's much too big, I'll grant you, and we never had children to use all that space, but we loved it. Dolores was a big entertainer, so it was ideal. Not so much anymore."

Marg knew she had changed after meeting Emile. Maybe it had with Emile, as well.

"What do you mean, not so much anymore?"

"It's more than just empty space, Marg. It's empty living, if you understand. Since Dolores died, there's no one there except me, and I'm not a great conversationalist or social organizer. Why do you ask?"

Both of them knew why she asked.

"How about we make both of us happy, Emile? Why don't you downsize to a condo? Even better, why don't I take on a roommate?"

"Do you have someone in mind, Marg?"

"I hear there's an older woman roaming the wilderness who needs a home and a lover and a companion. Not necessarily in that order, but you get the gist of it. She comes with one caveat, though."

Emile stiffened. Did she want control of his money?

"Apparently she'd like to be married. She's old-fashioned that way. You know how people talk and gossip about scarlet ladies."

Emile reached over and gave her a big hug. "I thought you'd never ask. Of course I will."

They both laughed uproariously.

"Emile, have you ever done anything impulsive? Have you ever seen a great opportunity and grabbed it without thinking?"

"Marg, you know me. Mr. Impulsive, that's who I am. Never have." They both laughed wildly. "Why do you ask?"

"The Blue Duck is closed tomorrow." She continued in a matter-of-fact way, "Let's get married and have a wedding reception there. Everybody is looking for something to do on a Sunday. This could be the greatest party Port Detour has ever seen."

Emile hadn't seen that coming. His mind went blank, his mouth hung open, but no words came out.

"Are you OK, Emile? Are you having a heart attack?"

His senses returned. "But, but we haven't even talked about this. Married?"

"Why not? It's impulsive, Emile, I'll grant you, but it's also right. Let's get on the phone and start inviting. It's be a brunch wedding and we'll get a disk jockey for the music."

Something must have snapped in Emile's brain. He grabbed Marg's hands and guided her to the centre of the living room and started dancing and singing. "I'm getting married in the morning. Ding dong, the bells are going to chime."

Marg buried her face in her hands. Then she started crying. "I'm so happy, Emile. Too bad you aren't." She laughed until tears of joy appeared.

It only took thirty minutes to make the calls. Nobody turned them down.

Chapter 44

A dark blue Japanese branded compact car rolled past Kendrick's and Floyd's houses around ten in the morning, finally easing to a stop at the end of the cul-de-sac, over fifty metres from the nearest house.

The driver stepped out, locked the doors, and clicked open the trunk. He was dressed like a hiker or hunter - boots, camouflage pants, a black T-shirt and light windbreaker. Around forty, of medium height, black slick backed hair and cleanly shaven, he could have been anybody's image of a fitness enthusiast. Mario reached into the trunk, pulled out a black canvas bag, and reassembled the Remington 783 high-powered rifle and telescopic sights. Finished, he threw the bag back into the trunk and retrieved a box of 180 grain bullets from the now empty bag. He checked the gun and sights, appeared satisfied that all was in order, slammed the trunk shut and set off on his hike, the rifle in his left hand.

No one was about late Sunday morning to observe his actions. He didn't care, anyway. He was just another hunter traipsing the hills around Sudbury, doing rifle practice in anticipation of the Fall moose hunting season. His path took him uphill to a spot directly behind Floyd's and Kendrick's houses, providing a full view of both houses and their back decks.

It was a glorious day, sunny and warm, and the slight chill and meagre hoarfrost from the night had vanished. Mario sat down, lit a cigarette, and waited.

The front doors of the Blue Duck Tavern were propped wide-open. Sunlight flooded the interior, the first time since it was built over fifty years ago. Marg and Emile stood at the entrance, greeting guests.

"Welcome, Forest. Welcome Gail, Great to see you, Dakari. Glad you could make it, Gert." The stream of guests from the parking lot was never ending. Everyone was dressed for the occasion, their previously reserved-for-Sunday best now transformed into party clothes.

"You were right, Marg. It's a great crowd. Should we open with a Bible reading?"

"Don't you dare, Emile. Somebody would get hurt in the stampede out the door and we wouldn't have any guests left." She laughed at her own joke. "However, turning water into wine would be handy." Another joke. Emile beamed at her. By God, she was happy.

Thirty minutes later, Emile put his hand on her arm and said, "I think that's everyone, Marg. Let's join our guests and get the music moving. I want to dance with the lady in red." Indeed, Marg was dressed in a brilliant scarlet dress which suited her skin colour and figure perfectly.

Emile stood in front of the crowd and whistled to get attention.

"This is Happy Sunday, and we want everyone here to have such a good time, no one will ever forget the marriage of Marg and Emile."

"First, the official part," said Emile, "and then party time. Our officiant today is an old friend of mine, from my police days. Please welcome Reverend Bob Fellows. He's going to make Marg and I official."

The ceremony only took ten minutes, the marriage papers were signed and Emile announced, "The bar is open." He waved at Kendrick, who was busy setting up champagne glasses at the bar in the centre of the room. "Let the music start." He waved at the disk jockey. "The first dance is mine, and it's with a gorgeous lady in red." He turned, held out his hand, and gently led Marg to the makeshift dance floor.

Emile held Marg in his arms and whispered into her ear. "This one's for you."

Chris DeBurgh's voice filled the tavern as the strains of Lady In Red gradually grew in volume. Marg, overwhelmed, couldn't hold back the tears. It was her favourite song.

Mario saw the two of them come through the kitchen sliding doors onto the deck. He lay down in a prone position, grabbed the rifle, checked that the magazine was full, and sighted on the two men. They appeared to be having a meal and a beer. Mario adjusted the rifle to the left and, with the powerful telescopic sight, could easily see that the person facing him was eating a sandwich. The crosshairs were positioned on his chest.

Breath slowly and regularly and then hold your breath, he told himself. He steadied the barrel, slowly moved his index finger and pulled the trigger. The sound of the shot reverberated throughout the rocky hills. A flock of eight or maybe ten large black crows took to the air, cawing loudly.

"Dad, Dad, what's wrong?" said Rollie as his father jerked backwards and then fell forward, not associating the sound of the rifle shot with what he saw happening. A pool of blood spread slowly across the picnic table. Rollie got up and ran around to lift his father up. Everet was not breathing.

"No, no, no," he cried. Instinctively, he raised his head and looked at where the sound of the shot originated.

Before Chris DeBurgh's last notes died away, the crowd reacted in unison and cheered wildly.

"This is one for the books," said Forest. "Who would have imagined those two getting together?"

"Just like you and I," replied Gail, envy in her voice. "We should do this too. What do you say, Forest?"

Forest's mind was busy calculating the cost.

"Gail, I know your favourite music. Let's get the disk jockey to play it." He looked at his live-in partner expectantly, hoping all thought of spending such an enormous amount of money now replaced with instant gratification.

"Oh, I'd love that, Forest. Go ahead, do it. Ask the disk jockey,"

Forest slowly walked over to the young man, furiously trying to confirm in his own mind just what was Gail's favourite song. He realized this was important, more important than he first thought. What was next? Marriage?

Maybe it was The Twist? No–too old. Then he remembered.

As the first notes sounded through the tavern, Gail turned to him, "You remembered Forest. I love you."

'I could have a mansion that is higher than the trees,' sang Crystal Gayle.

Mario quickly put another bullet in the chamber, sighted through the scope and was presented with the image of a young man, his face distorted in agony.

Interesting, he thought. I've never looked at the face of anybody I've killed before I pulled the trigger. The image disturbed him. Momentarily.

Again, he steadied the barrel, took a breath, held it and squeezed the trigger. Again, the sound of the shot reverberated throughout the rocks. The young man disappeared from his view.

The crows had settled in the nearest shrubbery after the first shot and were now on the move again. Absurdly, Mario tried to remember what a group of crows was called. Where that thought came from was a mystery,

Next door, Floyd heard the shots. Initially, he thought little of the sound. After all, many people living in Sudbury were hunters and the sound of rifle fire in the outlying areas was not usually a cause for alarm. It did sound close, he thought.

Now curious, he opened the sliding doors to his deck and stepped out.

"Rollie," he shouted, "did you hear that?" He walked out to the edge of the deck and looked up to the dark grey hills. The cawing of the crows filled the air.

Forest took Gail in his arms. "Just like you asked, my dear. I don't forget a thing about you." Forest swept Gail on to the dance floor.

"You old smoothy," exclaimed Gail. "You really know how to dance."

"Only one of my talents, my dear," said Forest. The inflection in his voice signalled nothing but happiness. Life is great, he thought.

The dance floor filled up rapidly, the bar was crowded, and everyone agreed that Sunday afternoon was just about the best time for a party. None of that late night stuff when everyone their age was trying to suppress a yawn.

Mario shifted his position slightly as he saw a person exit from the house next door. He checked the rifle again to make sure the chamber was loaded. He swung the barrel further to the left and an older person came into view of the telescope. Again the same routine, except with this one he had a clear view with no one else around the person. The crosshairs lined up and the second after he pulled the trigger, he could see Floyd crumple to the deck floor.

His job was done. His instructions were to leave no witnesses. He picked up the rifle, ambled back to his car, disassembled the weapon, and stowed it in the trunk. Within ten minutes of firing the last shot, he turned around and headed for Toronto. The crows still bothered him. What a group of crows was called would come to him on the road.

Once he was on Highway 69 south, he turned on his cell phone, brought up a number, and pressed the call button.

"Mario," the gruff voice at the other end said, "how's it going?"

"All done, boss. See you tomorrow." He hung up. The cash to pay Floyd was still in his pocket and the boss hadn't asked about it. Rarely do you get a bonus in his line of work.

Then it hit him. They were called a murder. A murder of crows, that was it.

Forest, Gail, Dakari, Rey Rey and Kendrick met the happy couple at the entrance as they left. Nobody wanted the party to end, but both Emile and Marg had to admit they were tired. It had been a whirlwind twenty-four hours,

"We'll probably see you tomorrow," said Marg to the group. "I've got to tell you, this has been the happiest day of my life. It's great to be alive."

Everyone nodded in agreement.

Dakari raised his half empty glass of champagne. He was the only one still drinking.

"I'll toast to that. Certainly beats the alternative."

Manufactured by Amazon.ca
Bolton, ON